ABSENCE MAKES
THE HEART

ABSENCE MAKES
THE HEART

LYNNE TILLMAN

British Library Cataloguing in Publication Data
Tillman, Lynne
  Absence makes the heart.
  I. Title
  II. Series
  823′. 914 [F]

  ISBN 1–85242-176–2

The pieces included in this edition have been previously published as follows: 'AKA Mergatroyde' in *New Observations*, 1985; 'The Trouble With Beauty' in *Conjunctions 14*, 1989; 'Other Movies' in the *Catalogue for the Binational* (Oct. 1988); 'Madame Realism's Imitation of Life' in *Fake*, New Museum catalogue 1987; 'Dead Talk', 1986, and 'Hung Up', 1984, in *Between C & D* magazine; 'A Nomadic Event in the Body' in *Semiotexte*, 1984; 'Absence Makes the Heart' in *Portable Lower East Side*, 1984; 'Living With Contradictions', *Top Stories*, 1982; 'Words Without Pictures' in *Bomb 4, 1982; the complete text of 'Weird Fucks' first appeared in Bikini Girl* magazine, 1980; 'Diary of a Masochist' was published anonymously in *Paranoids Anonymous Newsletter*, 1978; 'Madame Realism' was published by the author in an artist's book with drawings by Kiki Smith, 1984.

First published 1990 by
Serpent's Tail, 4 Blackstock Mews, London N4

Typeset in 10/12½ pt Walbaum by Selectmove Ltd, London
Printed on acid-free paper by
Nørhaven A/S, Viborg, Denmark

CONTENTS

For David Hofstra

WEIRD FUCKS

Chapter 1 There's a Snake in the Grass

I'm on my way, one of four NYC college girls, heading
for Bar Harbor, Maine, to spend the summer as a
chambermaid, waitress, or piano player. Bar Harbor
is on Mt Desert Island, linked with the mainland by
one bridge only and, we are warned, if there is a fire,
we might all be caught on the island. Only two lanes
out, they caution in dour Maine tones, and the only
way out.

Bar Harbor is full of Higginses. There are three bran-
ches of the family, no one branch talking to the other
two. We took rooms in Mrs Higgins' Guest House.
Willy Higgins, a nephew to whom she didn't speak,
fell in love with me. He was the town beatnik, an artist
with a beard and bare feet. He would beat at the door
at night and wake all four of us. I'd leave the bedroom
Hope and I shared to be embraced by this impassioned
island painter who would moan, 'I even love your dirty
feet.'

I was in love with Johnny. Johnny was blond and
weak, his mother an alcoholic since his father died
some years back. Johnny drove a custom-built racing car
which had a clear plastic roof. He was a society boy.

The days for me were filled with bed-making and toilet-cleaning. I watched the motel owner make passes at women twice my age who couldn't read. We had doughnuts together at six a.m. I would fall asleep on the beds I tried to make.

At night Hope would play cocktail piano in bars and I'd wait for Johnny. Mrs Higgins watched our comings and goings and spoke in an accent I'd now identify as cockney. She might have been on the front porch the night Johnny picked me up in his mother's station wagon. We drove to the country club in the middle of the night and parked in the rough behind a tree. We made love on the front seat of the car. I actually thought of F. Scott Fitzgerald. He asked me to put my arms around him again. He whispered in my ear that although he knew many people, he didn't have many friends. He asked if I minded making love again. This would be my third time.

The rich boys who were sixteen and devoted to us NYC girls robbed a clothes store in Northeast Harbor. They brought the spoils to our apartment. Michael, a philosophy student and the boyfriend of one of us, insisted the stuff be returned within twenty-four hours or else he'd call the cops. The next night Bill returned the tartan kilts and Shetland sweaters that hadn't been missed. But he dropped his wallet in the store while bringing it all back and somehow or other the cops were at our door the night after. They spotted me as the ringleader. We went to Bangor for our trial and got fined $25 each as accessories. They called it a misdemeanor. The newspaper headline read Campus Cuties Pull Kilt Caper. I didn't really want to be a lawyer anyway I thought.

Johnny never called again. I dreamt that Mrs Higgins and I were in her backyard. I pointed to a spot in the uncut lawn and said with alarm: there's a snake in the grass.

A guy who hawked at carnivals wanted me to join the circus and run away with him. I was coming down from speed and learning to drink beer. Some nights we'd go up a mountain and watch the sunrise. Bar Harbor is the easternmost point in America, the place where the sun rises first. I pined away the summer for Johnny and just before heading back to NYC heard that his mother had engaged him to a proper society girl.

Chapter 2 An East Village Romance

I was a slum goddess and in college. He looked something like Richard Burton; I resembled Liz. It was, in feeling, as crummy and tortured as that.

George had a late-night restaurant on St Marks Place. I'd go in there with Hope, my roommate; we'd drink coffee, eat a hamburger. Fatal fascination with G behind the counter – his sex hidden, but not his neck, his eyes, his shoulders. He called me 'Little One.' 'Little one,' he'd say, 'why are you here? What do you want?' I'd sit at the counter with hot coffee mug in hand, unable to speak, lips pressed on teeth, teeth pressed in heart, heart located in cunt, inarticulate. Michael said I was 'cunt breathing free.'

José was George's best friend and George had a Greek wife who was not around. The guys and I hung out together. $1 movies at the Charles. Two-way conversations between the artists (they were both sculptors) while I hung, sexually, in the air. José had a red beard, George had no beard, just greyish skin in the winter. 'Little One,' he'd say, 'what do you want?' He'd trace a line on my palm as if it were a map of my intentions.

Still, with so much grey winter passion, no fucking. Night after night, nights at the counter, count the nights. I met his wife who dried her long black Greek hair in the oven. They are separated. It is a recent separation and I am passionately uncaring. I am in love. I take trips with other people to places I can't remember. I spend hours talking with an older woman called Sinuway who gives me a mirror to remind me I am beautiful. She disappears.

José reminisced about the fifties when beatniks roamed the streets. In those days George made sidewalk drawings. One time José recounted, 'George was very drunk – very drunk, heh George – and drawing a young girl's portrait. For hours and hours because he'd fallen asleep behind the easel, his face blocked by the paper. Finally George collapsed at her feet, right on his face, nothing on the paper. Remember, George?' Stories like these passed the time. Weeks passed.

George, José and I were in George's room and José put a ring on my finger then left the room. George and I were alone. He undressed me and placed his hand on the place between my breasts. He undressed me in the doorway. He unbuttoned everything and fucked me. It went fast, after so many weeks, like a branch breaking off a tree. The time had come. It was a snap.

'I want to write a poem,' he said, his cock still hard. 'Oh, I don't mind,' I said, dressing as fast as I could. I wanted to be indifferent, not to burden him with my lack of sophistication. He had an ugly look on his face. Perhaps he was thinking about his recently separated wife drying her hair in the oven while he fucked a young woman.

Back at St Marks Place, I headed home, thinking that this might be reason for suicide. All that time, that perfunctory fuck, that poem he would write. It was all over. I phoned Susan who still lived at home; her life wasn't plagued with late night restaurants. 'What would you do,' I asked. 'Forget it,' she said, 'it's not important.'

Later that night Hope and I went out again and I met Bill. He traced a line from my palm up my wrist all the way to my elbow.

Chapter 3 A Very Quiet Guy

Bill and I left Hope and went to the Polish Bar not four doors from George's late night restaurant. Beer ten cents a glass. We drank and drank; I told Hope I'd be home soon and wasn't.

Somehow we were upstairs in somebody's loft. Bill had red hair and brown eyes. He was very tall and wore a flannel shirt. We made love all night long, this kind of sleepless night reassuring. His rangy body and not much talking. He'd keep tracing that line from my palm to my elbow, the inner arm. He disarmed me. It was easy to do.

Early morning at the B&H dairy restaurant, our red faces like Bill's hair. Breakfast with the old Jews in that steamy bean and barley jungle. Romance in the East Village smelled like oatmeal and looked like flannel shirts. Our smell in the smell of the B&H. George and José walk in and it was a million years ago, those weeks of grey passion and one snappy fuck. Sitting with Bill, so easily read, I smile at them. George looks guilty and embarrassed. I feel wanton and he is history.

Bill and I started to go together. He told me about his wife from whom he was separated. She was on the other coast. That seemed like a real separation. Bill was quiet and often sat in a corner. I thought he was just thinking. I introduced Michael, the first hippie I knew, to Nancy, my best friend. We spent New Year's together on 42nd Street, Nancy kissed a cop, the guys pissed on the street and Michael pissed in the subway.

Bill and I started a fur eyeglass-case making operation which I was sure would catch on. We convinced

Charley, owner of the fur store on St Marks Place, that those scraps of fur would make great eyeglass cases. A fur sewing machine was rented and placed in the basement of the fur store. Bill and I passed nights sitting side by side, silently, in old fur coats, stitching up cases which never did get sold. Bill grew more and more quiet.

My father had his first heart attack. The subways were on strike and I took long walks to Mt Sinai in my fur coat to visit my father in the intensive care unit. The first night he was in the hospital I couldn't go home. I slept on the couch at Nancy's mother's apartment. In the morning Nancy stood by the couch, anxious because the sheet covered me completely, like a shroud, and she wondered how I could breathe.

One night Bill fucked me with energy. Spring was coming and so was his wife, he told me later. I stormed out of the fur store, yelling that I would never see him again, and fumed to the corner where I stood, having nowhere to go. That fuck was premeditated – wife here tomorrow, do it tonight. I turned back and returned to Bill and Michael who said, 'We knew you'd be back. You're too smart for that.'

We went to Nancy's and suddenly I was sick, throwing up in her mother's toilet bowl. Bill held my head, my hair. He took me to my apartment and made me oatmeal. Left me propped up in bed with a pile of blankets and coats over me. Three days later, I awoke, my flu over.

His wife had a beautiful voice and was as tall as he was. And while I could get him out of my system he couldn't get out of the system. He didn't want to resist the draft; he desperately wanted to pass the tests, especially the mental test. When he received his notice telling him he was 1-A, he tried to kill himself. Slit his wrists. Last time I remember seeing him he was sitting in an antique store, rocking, near the window. We waved to each other.

Chapter 4 No/Yes

I threw caution to the wind and never used any contraception. Nancy finally convinced me I might get pregnant this way and made me an appointment at Planned Parenthood. It was a Saturday appointment and that night I had a date with John, a painter from the Midwest, a minimalist. So the doctor put the diaphragm in me and I kept it in, in anticipation of that meeting. Besides I had lied to the woman doctor when I said I knew how to do it – I was afraid to put it in or take it out. Let it stay there I thought, easier this way.

We met at the Bleecker Street Cinema and watched a double feature. Godard. Walked back to his place below Canal Street. We made love on his bed and he said, 'I'm sorry. This must be one of my hair trigger days.' 'What does that mean?' I asked. He looked at me sceptically. It was difficult, very difficult, for men to understand and appreciate how someone could fling herself around sexually and not know the terms, the ground, on which she lay. He said, 'It means to come too quickly.' 'Oh', I said, 'that's all right.' I kept comforting men. He fell asleep fast.

I awoke at three a.m. with just one thought. I had to get the diaphragm out. If it were possible and not already melted into my womb or so far up as to be near my heart or wherever diaphragms go when you're ignorant of where they can go.

I pulled a rough wool blanket around me and headed for the toilet in the hall. John awoke slightly and asked where I was headed. For a piss, I lied.

The heavy door opened into a dark hall. The toilet door opened, just a toilet and no light. I stood in the dark and threw my leg up on the toilet seat as shown in various catalogues not unknown to the wearer. Begin searching for that piece of rubber. Think about Margaret Sanger and other reassuring ideas. Can't reach the rim. Reach the rim; finger slips off. Reach it, get it and pull. Can't get it out. It snaps back into place as if alive. Go into a cold sweat. Squat and try. Finger all the way up. Pull. Then try kneeling. I'm on my knees with my finger up me, the blanket scratching my skin. It seems to be in forever. This is a Herculean task never before recorded. An adventure with my body. In forever.

I pulled the blanket up around me and stood, deciding to leave it in for now and have it removed surgically if necessary. In a colder sweat I left the dark toilet to return to the reason for all this bother. I couldn't pull the loft door open. It seemed to be locked or blocked. Began banging heavily against the metal door. Hot sweat now. When John finally opened the door he found me lying flat out on the blanket, a fallen angel, naked at his feet. I'd fainted. He revived me and we were both stunned. 'The door,' he said, 'was open.' That's what they all say. He gave me a glass of water and we went back to bed.

The next morning, even though he said our signs were right, my fainting has indicated other signs. Signs and more signs. I walked toward Canal Street and a sign on the wall read Noyes Electrical Company which I read No/Yes Electrical Company. No/Yes, I thought, that's a strange name for a business.

Chapter 5 An American Abroad

Rome was hot and strange in the summer. Nancy and I had been in Europe three weeks. We were tourists on the Spanish Steps. She met a Spaniard called Juan and

I met his friend called Ricardo. Ricardo and I didn't get along very well and he thought I was an 'egoist' as I tried out my college Spanish. All my sentences began with Yo and I was either tired, hungry or hot. Nancy and Juan began a five-year relationship which had her living in Yugoslavia for four of those years. Ricardo returned to Madrid.

Mao appeared one day at the steps. He was tall, thin and brown, a French Vietnamese. Suddenly he was my boyfriend and we were going to go to Greece together. Ours was a silent love affair and I'm not sure how we reached a decision like we were going to go to Greece together. My French was slightly worse than my Spanish, always akin to the pen of my brother is on. . . I believe we used interpreters, particularly when we fought. I discovered that I was sullen in both French and Spanish, but the languages, on my primitive tongue, seemed to lend themselves to moodiness.

Together, Mao and I did all the right things like eating in a poorhouse run by Franciscans and trying to get into one of the numerous movies being made in Rome. About fifty of us were taken on a forced march to a suburb outside Rome where Anita Ekberg or some other blonde star looked down on us from her balcony to single several of us out as looking like hippies. The rest of us were sent back to Rome, not right for the part.

Juan and Nancy wanted to sleep outside in the gardens of the Villa Borghese. Though I had a hotel room, Mao and I decided to join them. They disappeared behind a tree, some several yards above us on a small hill. Mao and I spread our blanket on the ground, took off our pants, made love and fell asleep. He was very beautiful and the lovemaking was nothing much at all.

It was a hot night and very still in the gardens. I awoke, feeling light shining down on me. There are lights shining on us, the headlights of a cop car. Two policemen are standing at the foot of our blanket. They shine flashlights. Mao stands up pulling on his trousers. I can't find mine, they're hidden somewhere and I try to pull the blanket around me as my hand feels the ground, looking for them. But those Italian cops are fast, fast to spot a piece of ass. 'Nuda. Nuda,' one yells, pointing at my ass as if I were already behind bars or in a zoo. My ass I figure is probably reflecting the light of the moon. I wonder if this image could ever be seen as romantic. The other echoes his cry: 'Nuda, Nuda.' Now we're in for it, I think, semi-nude fornicating hippies found in elegant Borghese gardens. An international incident.

I become hysterical, nuda nuda, still searching for my clothes. I find them, put them on and stand up behind Mao who is attempting to hide me from the cops. This gesture is futile and indeed ridiculous, as if Adam and Eve could hide from the authorities. They're not at all interested in Mao. I decide to play dumb. I point at my head and my chest, emphatically declaring, Stupido americana, stupido americana. I'm not at all sure of the agreement but I figure they'll get the point. And the point is that if I admit I'm an idiot, particularly an American idiot, Americans are hated in Europe, if I admit all this, they may go easy on me. Mao stands by the blanket. They lead me to the cop car. I'm being taken away.

They push me into the back seat of the car. One cop gets in the driver's seat and the other tries to slam the back door after me. I shove my leg out so that he can't close the car door, unless he wants to cripple me. I leap out of the car and go running into the night. I keep running and the cops don't follow, they just get back into their car and drive away.

Nancy had watched from safety, behind a tree. Said it was the funniest thing she's ever seen. Like a Keystone comedy. Mao and I continued to communicate badly with one another until I said something which hurt him deeply – something I never understood, perhaps it translated poorly – and he left Rome, or so a friend of his interpreted.

Nancy went off with Juan and someone who called himself a friend of Juan's, seeing me alone, offered me his sister's house as hospitality. I fell asleep in the front seat of his Mercedes as we drove away from Rome toward what I supposed were the suburbs. I awoke in the car which was parked next to a field. After he raped me, he said, 'Now we go to my sister's house.' It had seemed pointless to fight him off and then go running around the Italian countryside in the dark when I had had a taste of what the police were like. He thought, because I hadn't resisted, that I liked it.

Two days later I got out of Rome, following the sun to Greece, hitching with a sixteen-year-old English boy who carried my rucksack on top of his. On the Continent, only, can one trust Englishmen to be old-fashioned.

Chapter 6 Coming of Age in Xania

I was sitting on a sidewalk in Athens, sitting on the curb in front of a shoe store. Jack saw me and called out, 'Are you an American?' and I answered, 'Yes,' and told him I was looking for a hotel. 'Share mine,' he said, 'a dollar a night.'

Jack was from Chicago, a spoiled and wealthy Irishman who wanted to write. He had just gotten to Athens from Tangier. He had reddish hair, pale skin and eyes Carla would have called 'sadist blue.' He was recovering from an unhappy love affair which, having ended badly and to his disadvantage, made him vindictive and self-righteous. I didn't want to travel alone and he looked like a life-saver. We went to Crete and he hated me or at least it seemed that way. 'Look, Jack,' I told him, 'you can stay in the house I'm renting but our being together is insane since you criticize me constantly.' He didn't argue this point and we agreed to be housemates only. But Xania is a small city and a small Greek city at that and a young woman doesn't leave a man simply. Or at all. Friends of Henry Miller littered the island and all would later descend on me for my unfairness to Jack who was drinking so much now.

I had fallen in love with Charles who arrived with Betsy and her child. She was separated from her husband who had remained in their native land, South Africa. Charles told me that he and Betsy were friends. They seemed like adults to me, the big-time, and when Charles looked at me longingly, I returned the look. At first we were secretive. Betsy, who was older and probably wiser, seemed to take this in her stride and Charles moved out, into his own room near my rented house and Jack still slept in my bed and every night I would leave my house and go to Charles' bed. He wanted to be a writer too. Jack and I would have pleasant talks together on the terrace. We'd smoke some grass and he'd talk about his broken heart. Things seemed ok and in fact they were extremely bizarre.

The first week in Xania I was cast, in my naïveté, as the young thing who arrives in town and enters a world she doesn't understand. This was my screen role in Charles Henri Ford's film *Johnny Minotaur*. I had been given Ford's address by a Greek called Stephanos. He approached me on the Spanish Steps, urging me to go to Crete and look up Charles Henri. Luckily for Charles Henri who left Xania shortly after filming Jack and me in a classic beach scene – I wore a skirt and held a black doll in one hand, a pinwheel in another – he never saw his second heroine devolve into her role.

Xania is made for secretive strolls, its lanes curve from house to house. I took these turns recklessly, leaving my house every night, strolling a curved lane to Charles' bare room where we would lie together on the skinny cot. Morning would come and I'd stroll back to my house. Breakfast at the Cavouria restaurant and a swim before lunch. I took to going fishing and the fishermen would smile as I walked down the pier to the tower and cast my line into the sea. I never caught anything.

Betsy continued to be civil to me. We went dancing at a tavern where the Greek sailors did their famous carrot dance. Charles didn't come and I sulked. Betsy was understanding and her graciousness made me uncomfortable. We watched a sailor place a carrot at his crotch and another sailor hack away at it with a knife. I went to sleep outside the tavern in Betsy's car and woke to find Greek sailors peering through the car windows. I was driven home.

The strolls continued. Charles was good-looking, moody, given to short-lived enthusiasm and other things I can't remember. Jack and I socialized with Greek waiters. Waiters have always been partial to me – my mother has always said I had a good appetite. One such waiter took us for really good food in a place where men who looked like officers cracked plates over their heads even though this was then against the law. The waiter then took us to his home and fed us some plum booze that's thick like a hot night itself. Jack and I went home and I went for my usual stroll.

Several weeks later it was common knowledge that the waiter's common-law wife wanted to kill me. Alfred Perles, his wife, and Betty Ryan – the friends of Miller – all accused me of destroying Jack. It was the right time to leave.

The woman who took care of my rented, decrepit house and lived just across the lane offered to wash my hair and bathe me. I hadn't had a hot bath in two months. She heated the water in a huge black cauldron over a fire in front of her house. She sat me in a plastic tub. She even scrubbed my back. I felt she had some sympathy for me, and had watched, from her position in the chorus, other, similar young women.

There was no love lost. Charles slept at my house on my last night in Crete, Jack having sailed away, alone, almost nobly, a week before. I refused to make love with Charles, complaining of the heat and the bugs, and as a final indignity kept my underpants on and slept over the covers, while he slept beneath them. Charles and Michael, who had played Count Dracula in Ford's movie, drove me to the airport. On a similar ride one year later Betsy's husband who had come, I imagine, to win her back, would be killed in a car crash. I got back to Athens.

Chapter 7 A Pass for the Night

Jos and I had been living together eight months, first in London and then in Amsterdam, where he and I ran a cinema and a film cooperative. He was in Utrecht visiting his girlfriend and I was in our room, wearing my Victorian nightgown and suffering. It was as if I were still taking speed – couldn't sleep, the night was ragged and endless. It wasn't easy to find sleeping pills or tranquilizers in Amsterdam. The Dutch were more into natural drugs, like hash. Later heroin.

Piet was a painter who lived just around the corner; he had been in a Godard film, was travelled, had a French wife who often left him; he was tough. He might have some pills.

I threw my fur coat over my nightgown. It was winter. In Amsterdam one can visit unannounced. I put on a pair of old-fashioned shoes and headed out in the middle of the night. It was snowing, all white out, like my nightgown.

An American named Marty was with Piet. Both had similar reputations. It was odd to see them together. I had met Marty a week before on the night I'd received notice from Jos that he wanted to move out, that he wanted us to live separately. He loved me, he said. I knew from the loveletters left on our bed that Jos was fucking someone else. This is the stuff that tries our souls. Oh, we hadn't been happy. I felt I was being finished off, planed down. After his phone call, I went, unhinged, to Cathrine's, where Marty happened to be. I cried as if I knew him or as if he weren't there. Cathrine handed me a joint. Misery became an awful joke. 'Marty,' I laughed, 'do you know a man for me?' His response, and I can't remember it exactly, indicated he was a man. I couldn't understand why a man would want a woman in pain. I wasn't sophisticated about sadomasochism.

That was a week ago and here I am in Piet's studio with Marty, and I'm an inmate with a pass for the night. I kept on my heavy fur coat to hide my nightgown, which made my presence even more eccentric. We listened to Dylan's latest album. Piet didn't have any pills, just hash. Marty said, 'I like your shoes.' This was an erotic comment, slightly perverse from his lips. He said he wanted to photograph me. I wish he had. I would have liked a picture like that, in the same way that I've always wanted to steal one

of those US Post Office pictures of the Ten Most
Wanted.

He stayed till 5 a.m. We fucked. I was a ghost. He
left to return to his Dutch wife, to awaken in their bed.
I didn't care at all. 'Stay beautiful,' he called out as he
closed the door behind him. I stayed awake for several
more nights.

By the time Jos returned I had accepted my destiny,
the universe and his leaving our room. I wanted him
to go. He didn't. And then I accepted that too. Marty,
seeing Jos and me together, never flirted with me
again, though we remained friendly. I wasn't sure if
it was disinterest or respect for another man's territory.
I didn't really care either way. I was the one who finally
moved out of the room on the Anjelierstraat (Angel
Street). But that was not the end.

Chapter 8 Lies in Dreams

Breaking up is hard to do. After more than a year with
Jos, I went alone to Paris and London. Jos followed; my
parents and one of my sisters were in Paris but I didn't
introduce them to him. He wasn't supposed to be there.
I went to London and Jos and I lived together again,
briefly, in that city until we had to find another room.
Searching for a room in London proved too much for
our poor spirits; Jos returned to Holland.

I met James at a film festival in London, thought he
was an interesting man. He told me he was a poet and
a publisher and might publish my work. Since I had no
work to publish, I didn't pursue him. He pursued me.
One morning Jos left for Holland and that night James
was at my door. We went to see Warhol's *Bike Boy*.
James' uncanny instinct for the kill would reappear,
but not for another two weeks. He would come calling
and I'd never be at home. He'd leave word that he'd

been. I became interested and sent a postcard telling him I was going to New York and Amsterdam but would see him when I got back to London. I was blasé. That night James appeared and found me. This moment having built to a fevered pitch, it was love at the front door. Then we had some tea.

I had not remembered any of our previous conversations, held at the film festival. He told me that we had had a long discussion about why I could not watch Otto Muehl's film *Sodoma* in which an animal is killed, and at the same time I was not one of those who wanted to stop Muehl from making a live action in the theater itself.

That second but first evening we joined my friends Susan and David for dinner and a lecture at the Etherius Society. The Etherius Society's leader was Charles King, a medium who believed himself to be in direct contact with the Venutians.

Got stoned during dinner and dropped a Van Morrison album from quite a height onto the record player after being told 'one can do things better when stoned.' This reminded me of that line in Djuna Barnes' story about her sister, 'She sugared her tea from too great a distance.'

The Etherius Society held its meetings at the end of the Fulham Road and in the basement of what appeared to be an ordinary English house. London always gives the appearance of the very ordinary. The lecturer was dressed in a business suit. James and I were in no ordinary state. The audience was mixed – old, young, artists, housewives, and business-people. The lecturer spoke for two hours or what seemed a lifetime. James and I laughed without sound. Our faces were impacted with mirth and though the lecturer glowered at us as he spoke about the Venutians and the Martians, we really couldn't help ourselves. It was when the tape of Charles King's conversation with the head Venutian played that some awful gutteral sound came from me. 'Come in, come in, Venus,' King called. And the head Venutian answered, 'Nim Nim two two, Nim Nim two two, I can hear you, old chap.' The lecturer was furious now and James who was used to how ordinary English craziness is was able to control himself. The lecturer continued to stare straight at us and said, 'We are now going to say the Venutian prayer. The lights will dim. And I would like to say one thing. You can snigger at the Martians but you cannot laugh at the Venutians.'

And so we fell in love and that night slept side by side in a large bed while another man slept in another bed in the same room. We did not fuck. I felt we had anyway, that his body had moved into mine. And then he did move in. I met all the English concrete poets and learned to drink tea from morning to night. We invented Fluff, a kind of joke about how we were existing, which turned out to be our relationship. When we made love he refused to go down on me but wanted me to suck his cock. And when he looked at me I turned to lava.

I went to Amsterdam to tell Jos it was over. In true romantic fashion I did this from a sickbed; I'd sent him a telegram the day before saying that I was too ill to come to him. Jos came to me and sat on the edge of my bed for an hour as I spoke about why we couldn't go on. He was silent. (In the excess of my passion for James, I met another Englishman at one of Amsterdam's canals and we made love too. I threw away his telephone number and regretted this later.)

I returned to London and crazed days and nights with James. We shared a room on Lancaster Road near the Portobello Road. Our life was made of tarts, tea, cream and constant visits. One young man we visited, a poet, died the next year. His girlfriend later made love with James. I later made love with a close friend of James'. We all were trying to continue connections that had once been.

James wore a large wool robe and I wore a Japanese kimono that was always open to him. My thoughts were Spenserian; I was the true love and even if I were to go he would know the false from the true. I went to New York and stayed two months, sleepwalking around the city, seeing friends, going places, possessed. Nancy hardly knew me. I earned money to return and when I did, went to Susan and David's. They told me James had been acting very strange lately. So I phoned him and he hardly said hello. The next day he phoned me and asked me to come see him. He told me he was encased in glass. We spoke for more than an hour. He refused my presents and presence. He had gotten very thin and cut his hair short; he looked like a monk. I left his room and spent two months, waiting, in a Victorian nightgown. Anyone who has ever worn a Victorian nightgown knows its meaning, it is the gown of an inmate. I took valium and waited, would see James on the Portobello Road on rare walks out.

Over an Indian dinner a friend of his told me James was living with another woman. It was just after I'd bitten into a piece of food wrapped in silver paper. It was the beginning of the end of true romance, a fall that lasted two years.

I dreamt that I was with my father in my home town. We are driving around the Fox Estate. My father asks if I can settle down again and I say I don't know. Suddenly I am running wildly, wildly, down a wide path with trees lining each side. A man on horseback approaches and I leap out of the way only to hit a smaller horse, a pony, by the bigger pony's side. The pony drops to the ground. The man dismounts. My father reappears. The horseman looks very sad. 'He's not dead,' I cry, 'I merely hit him.' 'No,' the horseman says, 'he's not dead, but he is blind. We'll have to shoot him.' I scream.

I told James' friend the dream – he is the one I, woodenly, make love with in the future – and the friend said that there are lies in dreams too. I avoided speaking to people for a while.

Chapter 9 Suspicions Confirmed

By now everyone knows that valium is one way to get over a love affair. After taking those pills long enough, life becomes intensely fair: everything is the same. In this condition I visited friends and acquaintances with equanimity. Even people I didn't like. At one home I met Tim, a fringe Hollywood exile, actor, and public relations person for something or other. He was also a photographer. I met him and went home without expectation or particular interest, this being one of valium's cachets.

One week later the phone rang in the middle of the night. He said he'd been trying to reach me for a week, had even wired an office in New York at which he thought I worked. His enthusiasm only intrigued me.

He arrived with flowers and bought me steak. We got stoned and called his friend, a black man who seemed to represent to Tim all that is cool and noble in the world. Tim's friend invited us to his girlfriend's house outside London. We drove in the friend's car; I sat in back which was all right with me as I had become morose and paranoid. We were all very stoned too and I assumed we wouldn't arrive at the home of the ambassador from a small African nation. Tim's friend was seeing the ambassador's daughter. Sitting alone in the back seat of the car, I kept thinking that Tim's friend was driving sideways, that the road seemed to be giving way at every turn. I distrusted Tim inordinately. The driver was looking at Tim and not at the road. Their laughter encouraged my worst fears.

We arrived at the ambassador's house and were introduced to many children. The girlfriend was the eldest daughter. As if following protocol, she led us to the basement which had been converted into a game or conference room. It was filled with six over-sized leather lounge chairs. Like every ambassador's daughter I've ever met she had been educated in a French convent. The four of us sat in chairs much too big for us. I grew more and more alarmed. I hadn't the slightest desire to fuck Tim but there seemed no way out. There was an inevitability about the night. I was being driven places I didn't want to go. The mode was ineluctable.

Tim's friend drove us back to the city and dropped us at my place. We smoked some African grass and as I looked at Tim he became recognizable. 'You look,' I said, 'like my father's charcoal grey Perry Como sweater.' He looked at me quizzically but still advanced. I couldn't understand why, I thought my remark devastating.

Tim's stupidity was dangerous. When finally we were fucking, he was given to calling out, 'That's some cunt. That's some cunt.' In my condition his love-talk became absurd exaggeration. He made too much of a good thing (I thought). His enthusiasm grew as I retreated inside, and as if to draw me out, to reach me, he whispered bloodlessly, 'I'd like to kill you with my cock.' That was it. I knew it – in bed with a dangerous maniac who wants to kill me with his cock. All my suspicions were confirmed. This whole evening I was hanging on the edge of the fence, rigid with suspicion that was now given credence.

I drew back from his embrace and looked at his eyes which had narrowed. 'That's horrible,' I said, 'I can't continue.' It was impossible to prove to him that I was not crazy. The blind leading the blind and other such homilies come to mind. Besides I was in no position to argue.

It turned out that the wife I didn't know about was coming back from her vacation and I wouldn't have to see Tim ever again. When he left the next morning he gave me his sweater to keep.

Chapter 10 Just an Accident

I was staying away from men and lived and worked in Amsterdam where I found it easy to do so. A Dutchman let me use his back room and I camped there for the good part of a year. The Dutchman was depressed and cynical. I knew he wanted me to leave and when Carla suggested I join her and George Maciunas for a trip around the Greek islands (George wanted to buy one), I had to get there. Jos found me some money, a six hundred guilder scam, and I went by train to Greece. Three days and two nights on the Athens Express in a compartment with a Greek man from Thessaloniki who fed me feta cheese, bread and olives until he detrained. I read Jane Austen while on the train and feared that I might have to marry the Greek man, as several Greek women would pass our compartment and give us knowing smiles. I'm not one not to smile back and was relieved when he got off at Thessaloniki and I was not with him.

Carla and I settled again in Xania and she left before I did. I got very brown and into a little trouble, saying goodbye only because my money had run out.

I returned to Amsterdam.

Jack Moore once said, 'We are all going to be in Munich for the 1972 Olympics.' I nodded, 'Oh, yes?' and found myself there in the summer of 1972, along with twenty or more actors in Jack's theater company, The Human Family.

The hill of garbage, the rubble from World War II outside Munich since the postwar clean-up, is the site of the Olympiad. An artificial lake separates the games from the Spielstrasse, play street, where artists from Western Europe, Japan and America are to perform. The lake is polluted. The Olympics committee spent millions of marks to make Kultur at the games.

The Human Family was a participation theater group, using films, music, video and slides. I helped organize the production and directed some of the films. In Munich I also became a performer in the theater group, something I would ordinarily never do, having a horror of appearing in public, on a stage, but this was an extra-ordinary situation, more surreal than the Meret Oppenheim *Fur Teacup and Saucer*. I wrote postcards to friends, extolling this quality, and mentioned the thighs of the athletes.

The Spielstrasse abounds with German romantics who never die. Every tourist has some piece of equipment about the neck, arm or back. Busloads of varying nationalities embark, disembark, to watch theater pieces, clowns, conceptual artists, and then cross back over the polluted lake to see the games.

The German romantic I met was called Karl. He was political, did yoga seriously, and ate macrobiotic food. We spent several evenings in The Human Family's common room. Karl blew in my ear for three hours.

Each night our company performed its theater. Our piece began on the top of the hill and we ran downhill with a flashlight in each hand, waving our arms in the shape of the infinity symbol. I spent a good part of each day anxiously awaiting the run downhill. Even with our flashlights on, I was certain we couldn't be made out and I was afraid of rolling down the hill. But my fear about rolling downhill was small compared to what I felt about jumping onto the stage and going into slow-motion. We were wearing overalls too. Twenty of us in grey uniforms. After moving very slowly, we were to stare out at the audience which should have gathered at the foot of the stage. From this bunch each of us was to choose a person to encounter and bring up on stage with us. It was for me the worst kind of popularity contest. At the end of the piece we handed out donuts – the piece is also known as the Donut piece – and everyone danced around gaily to Shawn Phillips music written especially for the production. Our groups got a reputation for being very high, happy people, and many times other Spielstrasse workers joined us for the dance.

Charley was one such person. It took me some time to consider Charley seriously. Thinking in the midst of the Olympics and when a member of a theater group that makes donuts its symbol, thinking was hardly possible. Charley just entered my life. He smiled a lot and so did I. On the day the Israelis were murdered Charley came to see me, the rest of the company having gone to the country. We spread all the pillows on the floor and started to fool around. The door opened and three members of the West Indian steel band which lived rhythmically across the lane walked in. We were both naked and the men stood over Charley and me. They seemed to have no intention of leaving. What with our group's easy-going reputation on the Spielstrasse, this might have been expected. We asked them to go and they did. A few minutes later one came back and asked if he could be next. That's the way it began.

The Spielstrasse was closed because of the political situation but the games were allowed to continue. All the theater groups and artists met to protest the way in which Kultur was treated; the meetings ended in futility. The Japanese director Terayama and his group which performed only in black, red and white succeeded in getting back on to the play street. They started a fire and burned down their set. The flames could be seen for miles.

Everyone was going home. Charley asked if he could come with me to Amsterdam. I was surprised. Even more surprised when I discovered he was nine years younger than I was. And he already had a child whose mother was a smart and crazy amphetamine-head. They lived in Paris. So we returned to Amsterdam and lived and worked together for more than a year. I hadn't lived like this for some years and it was healthy to be fucking regularly. But Charley and I never did have much to say to each other. One day he came to me and said we shouldn't live together anymore; I lost him to a commune and his best friend whom I couldn't stand to be around. It was hell for a couple of months and when the hell was over, I rarely if ever thought of him again. This alone struck me as demeaning. A physicist once told me that one view of our universe is that its stability is an accident, that thousands upon thousands of relationships are unstable and that chance alone holds ours together.

Chapter 11 Lean Times

Watching an English television play reminds me of life with Graham, an English actor I lived with for two months. Charley and I had split up, work at the film cooperative was impossible – no one cooperated. The book I'd finished editing a year before still wasn't published and into this hole came an English acting company. The play they brought to Amsterdam was adapted from a novel a friend had written and the author being a friend, the cast became friends too. Of course no one makes friends that easily.

It was Edward whom the author told me to look up but I looked instead at Graham who was playing pinball after the play. It was, oddly enough, Valentine's Day. Two years before I'd written a short story on this day about the day and this year I found myself falling in love again. It is safer to stay indoors.

Three nights later Graham and I walked around Amsterdam, drinking in several bars, walking around and around. The way one can in Amsterdam, the city having been built in a semicircle. 'Not tonight,' I told Graham. We ended up at four a.m. in an Indonesian fast-food joint on the Leidesplein and ate peanut-covered meat. Shaslik.

Economics affects our life specifically: I had no money and no place to live since leaving the film cooperative. I had been living off the fat of the land and now, further into the seventies, there wasn't so much excess. Everything was getting tighter. After all those flowers and assassinations, optimism had died and business, of course, went on as usual. Lean times. Graham had a small house in London and a rented cottage in the English country.

Our third night in Amsterdam we smoked and ate some hash. We took a walk and as we walked I felt we weren't getting anywhere. There may be no progress, but still I felt we weren't moving at all. Graham was staying in a small hotel, the one set aside for English actors when they came to Amsterdam. They came often – Dutch theater is lamentable. He said as we got closer to the hotel, 'How are we going to get to my room?' The usual question of getting past the room clerk. With all the wisdom I could muster I replied, 'We'll just walk up the stairs.' Graham was amazed at this profundity, so simple, so direct, and indeed the way to his room was just past the room clerk and up one flight of stairs. The route to Graham himself was not so direct.

The next morning he left the hotel to stay at Elsa's house. I couldn't tell from the way Graham described Elsa and her situation if he was in love with her or she with him. In any case he described her primarily as a friend and an older woman, as if that would invalidate her. Later she and I became friends, and Graham's deviousness was reflected in phrases like 'an older woman.' It was hard for me to fuck Graham with Elsa below us in her solitary bed. The next night Graham agonized about whether or not we could make it with each other.

That Graham would leave town soon made our week intense, sweet. There's nothing like the promise of absence to make presence felt. When he left my bed to cross the Channel, Charley came to me and asked me to live with him again. We could squat a house, he said. I figured his coming to me had to do with smell but he was two weeks late and I wanted to get the hell out.

Spring in London. I filmed Graham in Hyde Park and in the garden. I baked apple pies, wrote poems about making apple pies – rhyming pie with die – and took to watercolors again. What an interesting couple we made. We went to his cottage in Norfolk. Listened to Stevie Wonder on the radio and I wrote letters about cricket, actors, country life; my letters were shaped with Jane Austen in mind, she being my model for the genteel English country life. The English have got cottage life down, like having tea at four. We visited the neighboring Lord and had a discussion about tied cottages. The pound may have dropped as we spoke.

We returned to London. I took a job in the neighborhood, making twenty pounds a week for a five-day
regime. And we shared the cost of living together.
I continued to cook. Susan visited from Amsterdam
and noted that she thought I was playing house. I was
very serious when I played, though. Graham thought
my friends were weird and I thought his superficial.

My book was up in the air and my plan was to return
to Holland, read the proofs, and come back to Graham
and our routine life. Graham's heart, about which I
heard a great deal, made it hard for him to be honest.
He never wanted to hurt anyone. And while he liked
me, he was still in love with the one before me. The
day I left for Holland she moved right back in. Graham
didn't let me know this, his heart was so big, for months
and months.

I went to Eastern Europe with my sister, happy to
be away, unhappy about Graham, again returning to
Amsterdam. Graham called, after those months had
passed, to give some apologies. Still later we held a
conversation that clarified matters further. He thought
because I had posed in the nude for a drawing course
and had worked on a sex paper, he thought I would
introduce him to the mysteries.

Chapter 12 Going to Parties

Living in New York City and going to parties. The last
ritual, attending parties. Katy introduces me to Steve
who is kneeling and I kneel too. My knees begin to hurt
and I stand over him. I'm sure he's queer with his Lou
Reed hair, overalls and big glasses. I watch him dance.
Not bad. I lose everyone I know and Steve and I begin
to dance. He's very tall and I can't see his face which
is hidden anyway by his glasses. The masked man. A
bad song comes on and we lean against the wall. 'Let's

go to my place,' he says, 'and we'll come back in a little while. It's real close.' That's friendly, I think, and say ok and off we walk in area unfamiliar to me. His loft is farther than a few blocks and it's raining. Maybe he's not homosexual.

The loft is six flights up and I begin by bounding the stairs two at a time. 'Take it easy,' he says, 'there's a lot more.' I enter the loft panting. My eyes are attuned to small Dutch quarters and the amount of space he has makes us both look small, insignificant.

Steve turns on The Wailers and we continue dancing. It's that movie when the dance becomes The Dance. He says, 'You were making eyes at me.' I tell him I wear glasses. We're lying on the bed. By now I realize he's heterosexual and this is the fashion. 'Are you Katy's boyfriend?' I ask, suddenly. 'Not anymore,' he says, 'we're both hot to trot.' I'm not sure what anything means and insist, drunkenly, that we go back to the party. He thinks I'm upfront. 'Since we're not going to fuck,' he says, 'wanna see my sculpture?' And next find myself seated inside a vibrating box.

Everything seems very funny. I feel both innocent and wild. 'Hey, little girl, you don't have to hide nothing no more. You haven't done nothing that hasn't been done before.' Katy walks up to me, 'you've been with Steve?' 'Yes,' I say, 'what about it?' She clears the decks and not only clears them but also indicates she has aimed me at him. 'He's a good fuck,' she says, and walks off. Is he or am I being passed on? There's something bloodless in the modern age.

Steve watches the discussion and says, 'I coulda hit you for talking to Katy.' 'Look, it's funny, Steve, don't you see?' We're dancing again, nearer to the wine and a Puerto Rican woman who really dances and I dance with her and smoke some grass and get given hash and Steve walks up and says (again), 'Let's go.'

We do the same walk, in the same night, up all those stairs, but there's a difference. 'Harder this time,' he says. Of course, I think. His roommate is at the far end of the loft. I know he's there but can hardly see him. More California wine and the television on by our heads. My head is turned toward it but I am not watching. Pulling off our clothes, on the bed, he thinks I'm watching the movie. I am and I'm not. It's just on, a forties movie, and it fits right in, somehow, with everything else. The guy at the far end of the loft is snoring. Steve and I are fucking. 'Did you come?' he asks. 'Not this time,' I answer. 'Next time,' he says. 'I trust you,' I say. But I can't sleep. The wine, grass, and sex. Parched throat. Water. Need water. 'Get me some too,' he says. It's dark and I take the long walk down the naked loft. That naked walk to get a glass of water. For a piss, or for water, so familiar in unfamiliar territory. Don Juan should see me now, gait of the warrior in a New York city loft. I find everything and return carrying two full glasses of water. I hand one to Steve. Cold water hits him in the face and he thinks I did it purposely. 'You bitch,' he says, just like in a forties movie. Then I know. He wants that. He keeps calling me Bitch. There's something refreshing about this reversal: a masochistic man. 'No,' I say, 'I wouldn't do that, pour cold water on you in bed.' Is this a concentration camp date?

I can't sleep and he's fast asleep. Why can they always sleep? Are men better sleepers? Big article: Men Superior to Women as Sleepers. The windows bang heavy during the night. A storm. The rain bangs against the windows. I look at Steve, closely now. No hair, no glasses. He looks like a little baby and has a small mouth. By the light of the storm, he looks like an alien. A young alien. I have to stop this and sleep. I know more about his cock than his face. Big cock, small mouth. The sun is coming in through the windows and I'm watching it. The light is dark as the rain continues.

In the morning Steve tells me he's into being macho. 'How do you mean?' I ask. 'Well,' he says, 'it's sort of feminism for men.' I tell Steve I have an appointment, which seems like a lie but isn't. With whom he asks. Sally, I say. Sally Blank? he is incredulous. Yes I say. 'She's a good fuck,' he reports. 'This is just like high school,' I say. 'Oh,' he goes on, 'and you don't know all of it. Anyway, Katy is using this material for her novel. She uses the gossip.' Well, at least that isn't new. He calls me bitch again as I dress and then he undresses me and my belt buckle makes a clumsy sound in the big, empty room. 'Why didn't you start this before I got dressed?' I ask. 'You moved too fast,' he says. His big hand touches, hardly touches my cunt, and we fuck again, not drunk or stoned. Lots of light now. 'You feel so good,' he says, 'and I have to piss.' He gets out, gets up and goes to piss. Stay for pancakes. Can't I stay.

He walks me to the door, wearing a terry cloth robe that just barely covers his tight ass. Lifts me high, kisses me and unlocks the door. It's pouring outside.

Some months later, we've remained friends, Steve asks how he can meet a woman. 'I'm confused,' he says. 'That's it,' I say. 'What?' he asks. 'That. Just let her see you're vulnerable. It works every time. Women are suckers for sensitive men.' The advice works. I'm invited to his loft dancing-wedding party a year later. The bride and groom wear dark colors and both have closely cropped hair.

Chapter 13 The Fourth of July

I should have known better. Upper middle class guys from Westchester are trouble and can't fuck. But look at that I say to myself, he's in therapy, talks about his mother with affection, wants to know something about me. The modern man aware of female independence. I'm not attracted to him though he's handsome in a way I find reprehensible – slick, well-dressed, clean but sweats a lot. Still he's so normal. The bait taken, Josh beat at my conditioned barriers and I let him in.

It's my first Fourth of July in the USA in seven years. And it's the Bicentennial at that. I'm not sure what people are celebrating but Americans like parties. We watch fireworks from a roof on Canal Street. The approach to the roof is the most dangerous aspect on this pacific evening. For while Amy had predicted bombs and I dutifully warned Sidonie, a French friend, to stay off the streets, five million people walk around Lower Manhattan, watch the tall ships, and eat. I eat Polish sausage and drink German beer.

The party begins tentatively as most do. But it is the Fourth of July and people want to have a good time. The dancing starts slowly and builds up, people secreting into the group one by one, then two by two. Martha knocks herself out on this hot night doing an energetic lindy then she disappears. A man with a moist face approaches me from behind and asks me to dance. There's something about being asked to dance that takes me back to sixth grade parties. Being asked to dance in this way and by a stranger is so American and perfectly right for the Fourth of July. He's sweating which keeps me at arm's length until he asks serious questions which soften me to him. I dance with him for a while but dismiss myself graciously, saying I'm going to the bathroom. I want to find Sidonie and see if she'd be interested in this earnest man, in Josh.

Red, white and blue chalk marks are drawn on my forehead. It's not the mark of Cain but still one can't help making an association like that. Judy has lines over her mouth, more like a clown. Things seem to be heating up with old lovers walking in and out, the party filling democratically with people one wants and one does not want to see. I introduce Sidonie to Josh but she's not interested and neither is he. It's not that easy. We dance again and he leaves, giving me a kiss on the cheek and the ritualized 'I'll phone you.'

Patsy and I do a vicious dance, a tango of sorts; the time is right for dancing in the streets and movements such as these. I tell Steve that this week he is not one of my favorite people and he takes this seriously, so we don't speak for months.

Firecrackers keep popping off and everything feels slightly evil. For the urban dweller whose adventures are limited to sexual ones the Fourth of July has nothing to do with America's independence. One's own independence being severely circumscribed anyway, we play out the hunt we can in limited ways.

Josh phones two nights later when I had all but forgotten him. His voice is reassuring and certain. We meet the next night at a Chinese restaurant, joined by Martha and her friend Don. Martha and Don are blond and fairskinned, Josh and I are dark-haired and tan.

Alone in a bar we talk familiarly about recent problems and the women he used to live with. This is the usual fare. I am still not attracted to him but consider this my failing. I tend toward men who aren't as nice. He says, 'But, we haven't talked about your writing.'

And he walks me home and since I have not changed my feelings toward him, I don't want him to go out of his way for me. He insists that he is doing what he wants to do. This kind of statement comes right out of therapy and I recognize it – he's taking responsibility for his actions. Still he strikes me as trying to be sensible. We walk to my street near Wall Street, talking all the way, and he invites me to a party the next night. By now he knows I'm leaving for San Francisco in a few days. This has created for him an urgency to see me more. I don't distrust this. I ask if I can bring Sidonie to the party and he says, 'Yes, of course.'

The party is on the Bowery. We pass alcoholics fighting over shoes. Across the street from his friend's party, there is a fire in a flophouse. It's like leaving a war zone when we enter the party. The men and women are spotless and fashionable and they are artists. Lots of good food and drink. The discrepancy can be watched, like a movie, out the window. A few drinks and I begin to appreciate Josh because he is so very attentive. This is a form of flattery that is most convincing, particularly at a party. When I was fourteen I discovered that boys would fall in love with me if I listened to everything they said. A strong sense of integrity prohibited me from continuing this form of seduction. And, in addition to integrity, there was the problem of having to continue to listen to them.

We dance and I still don't want to make love with him. I get drunker in order to overcome my disinclination, even disgust at the prospect. I am sure I don't want him because he's so nice, is like the boys I grew up with, and so openly likes me. I feel trapped. And it's kind of comfortable.

We get back to his loft and I see his paintings which are done from the back. This interests me because it is in sharp contrast to his regular guy demeanor. 'You're less open than you appear,' I say to him, surprising him with this insight. I immediately forget it, as if it were only academic, and sit on the couch beside him. Noticing my reluctance he thinks I'm nervous about making love with him for the first time. This amuses me inwardly but I cannot share my amusement with him. He begins to talk about 'the situation' and I know I'll either do it or I won't so I say, 'Let's go to bed.' A lot of performers get on the stage like that, just jumping on. Besides, I think to myself, this is an act I know with and without feeling. I am trying to get over a reluctance, the reason for which I do not know. The mechanics of sex make it easier for a woman to betray herself, which leads perhaps to her having different feelings about sex from a man whose sex organ is always a sign. We make love and once it's over I feel relieved, like having gone to the dentist and not having too many cavities. Perhaps needing only to have one's teeth cleaned.

When we awaken in the morning, I feel like talking, not rushing from his bed. By this time I'm involved – in something. Uninspired sex can win a masochist. It certainly makes sex not at all central to the relationship; it's so easy to forget. And so I felt that I really liked him and was not just attracted to him. Here is Puritanism, liking someone because the sex is bad.

I'm excited about leaving New York and having met a nice guy I can introduce to my friends. So I introduce Josh to lots of my friends, feeling certain and calm. He says I can phone him collect whenever I want. He phones me every week I'm away and I send romantic cards. I'm away for five weeks and don't make love with anyone else, partly out of this strange loyalty I develop like a rash when rubbed by certain kinds of men, partly because San Francisco didn't abound with men I could make love with. This combination appeared to be fate. Fatal.

When I get back to New York City, it is still hot. I phone him, leaving a message on his machine. He calls later and we meet that night. Everything seems to be going as it should. But he can't get it up. Says he is anxious about a show coming along faster than he expected. There's nothing to do about impotence except be understanding. But it was awful and not at

all like the dream I had of my return to New York —
he had made a painting which, when shot with a water
pistol, moved in mysterious ways we call orgasmic.

We both bury the lack of lovemaking as if it's just one
of those things. Josh asks me to go to the Hamptons
with him for the weekend but when I phone the next
day to find out when we're leaving, he begs off, and
says he wants to be alone. That he'll call me when he
returns. Says there's nothing wrong between us.

Sunday night passes, and Monday, it could've been
a long summer weekend. Josh never calls and I am the
one, finally, to call him. He speaks to me as if I were a
foreigner, a greenhorn who has the wrong expectations
about America.

One year later he comes up to me in a bar and,
smiling, asks, 'How are you and what are you up to
now?' I look at him blankly and answer 'The same.'
'You're distant,' he says to me, as if surprised, even
hurt by my disdain. He hadn't been a one-night stand,
a temporary shelter like a glassed-in bus stop on a
busy, rainy city street. Anonymous and more or less
alienating, or sexy, depending upon one's mood. He
had attenuated the one-night stand into something
more difficult to get over. For a while I was meaner
in the clinches, not so easy to fool. There are some
things I just won't forgive.

DEAD TALK

I am Marilyn Monroe and I'm speaking from the dead.
Actually I left a story behind. I used to be jealous
of people who could write stories, and maybe that's
why I fell in love with a writer, but that doesn't explain Joe. Joe had other talents. I didn't even know
how famous he was when we met. Maybe I was the
only person in America who didn't. I was glad he
was famous, it made it easier for a while, and then
it didn't matter, even though we fit together that way.
The way men and women sometimes fit together. It
doesn't last. I got tired of watching television. Sex is
important but like anything that's important, it dies
or causes trouble. Arthur didn't watch television, he
watched me. People thought of us like a punchline
to a dirty joke. Or maybe we had no punchline, I
don't know. Anything I did was a double entendre. It
was different at the beginning, beginnings are always
different.

Before I was Marilyn Monroe, I felt something shaking inside me, Norma Jean. I guess I knew something
was going to happen, that I was going to be discovered.
I was all fluttery inside, soft. I was working in a factory
when the first photographs were taken. It was during

the war and my husband was away fighting. I was alone for the first time in my life. But it was a good alone, not a bad alone. Not like it got later. I was about to start my life, like pressing my foot on the gas pedal and just saying GO. And the photographs, the first photographs, showed I could get that soft look on my face. That softness was right inside me and I could call it up. Everything in me went up to the surface, to my skin, and the glow that the camera loved, that was me. I was burning up inside.

Marilyn Monroe put her diary on the night table and knocked over many bottles of pills. Some were empty, so that when they hit the white carpeted floor they didn't make a sound. Marilyn made a sound for them, something like whoosh or oops, and as she bent over she pulled her red silk bathrobe around her, covering her breasts incompletely so that she could look down at them with a mixture of concern and fascination. Her body was a source of drama to her, almost like a play, with its lines and shapes and meanings that it gave off. And this was something, she liked to tell her psychiatrist, that just happened, over which she had no control. After three cups of coffee the heaviness left her body. The day was bright and cloudless and nearly over. She thought about how the sky looked in New York City, filled with buildings, and how that was less lonely to look at.

Marilyn just wanted to be loved. To be married forever and to have babies like every other woman. Her body, in its dramatic way, had other ideas. Her vagina was too soft, a gynaecologist once told her, and Marilyn imagined that was a compliment, as if she were a good woman because her vaginal walls hadn't gotten hard. Hard and mean. But maybe that's why she couldn't keep a baby, her uterus just wouldn't hold one, wouldn't be the strong walls the baby needed. Marilyn's coffee cup was next to her hand mirror and she was lying on her white bed looking up at the mirrored ceiling. She was naked now, which was the way she liked to be all the time. When she was a child, the legend goes, she wanted to take off all her clothes in church, because she wanted to be naked in front of God. She wanted him to adore her by her adoring him through her nakedness. To Marilyn love and adoration were the same.

Marilyn took the hand mirror and opened her legs. Her pubic hair was light brown and matted, a real contrast to the almost white hair on her head, which had been done the day before. It was as if they were parts of two different bodies, one public, one private. *My pubic hair is Norma Jean, how I was born,* she once wrote in her diary. It was hot and the air conditioner was broken. She could smell her own smell, which gave atmosphere to the drama. Her legs were open as wide as they could go and Marilyn placed the mirror at her cunt and studied it, the opening into her. Sometimes she thought of it as her ugly face, sometimes as a funny face. She made it move by flexing the muscles in her vagina.

He said he'd marry me but now I know he was lying. He said I should understand his position and have some patience. After all he has children and a wife. I told him I could wait forever if he just gave me some hope.

Marilyn took the hand mirror and held it in front of her face. She was thinner than she'd been in years. Her face was more angular, even pinched, and she looked, finally, like a woman in her thirties, her late thirties. She looked like other women. The peachiness, the ripeness that had been hers was passing out of existence, dying right in front of her eyes. And she couldn't stop it from happening. Even though she knew it was something that happened to everyone, it was an irreparable wound. Her face, which was her book, or at least her story, did not respond to her makeup tricks. In fact, it betrayed her.

Marilyn needed to have a child, a son, and she wanted him with the urgency of a fire out of control. Her psychiatrist used to say that it was all a question of whether she controlled Marilyn or Marilyn controlled her. Marilyn always fantasized that her son would be perfect and would love her completely, the way no one else ever had.

Sometimes I meet my son at the lake. One time he was running very fast and seemed like he didn't see me. I yelled out Johnny, but at first he didn't hear. Or maybe he didn't recognize me because I was incognito. He was so beautiful, he looked like a girl, and I worried that he'd have to become a fag. Johnny said he was running away from a girl at school who was driving him crazy because she was so much in love with him and he didn't care about her at all. I asked him if she was beautiful and he said he really hadn't noticed. Johnny told me every time he opened his mouth to say something, she'd repeat it. Just staring at him, dumb like a parrot. As his mother I felt I had to be careful, because I wanted him to like women, even though I didn't trust them either.

Marilyn had asked her housekeeper to bring in a bottle of champagne at five every afternoon, to wash down her pills. And because champagne could make her feel happy. Mrs Murray knocked very hard on the door. Marilyn was so involved in what she was thinking about, she didn't hear. Marilyn was envisioning her funeral, and her beautiful son had just begun crying. There were faces around her coffin. But his was the most beautiful. No, Mrs Murray said, he hadn't telephoned.

I told Johnny that more than anything I had wanted a father, a real father. I felt so much love for this boy. I put my arm around him and pulled him close. I would let him have me, my breasts, anything. He looked repulsed, as if he didn't understand me. He had never done this before. He had always adored me. Johnny wandered over to the edge of the lake and was looking down intently. I followed him and stared in. He hardly noticed me, and once I saw again how beautiful I was, I felt satisfied. Maybe he was too old to suck at my breasts. But I wanted, even with my last breath, to satisfy his every desire. As if Johnny had heard my thoughts, he said that he was very happy just as he was. He always lost interest anyway when someone loved him.

The champagne disappointed her, along with her fantasy. Deep down Marilyn worried that they had all lied to her. They didn't love her. Would they have loved her if her outsides had been different. No one loved Norma Jean. She could hear her mother's voice telling her, Don't make so much noise, Norma Jean, I'm trying to sleep. But it was Marilyn now who was trying to sleep, and it was her mother's voice that disturbed the profound deadness of the sleep she craved. If she couldn't stand her face in the mirror, she'd die. If they stopped looking at her, she'd die. She'd have to die because that was life. And they were killing her because she needed them to adore her, and now they wouldn't.

I hear my mother's voice and my grandmother's voice, both mad, and they're yelling, Save yourself, Norma Jean. I don't want to be mad. I want to say goodbye. You've got my pictures. I'll always be yours. And now you won't have to take care of me. I know I've been a nuisance and sometimes you hate me. In case you don't know, sometimes I hate you too. But no one can hate me as much as I do, and there's nothing you can do about it, ever.

Her suicide note was never found. Twenty years after Marilyn Monroe's death, Joe DiMaggio stopped sending a dozen roses to her grave, every week, as he'd done faithfully. Someone else is doing it now. Marilyn is buried in a wall, not far from Natalie Wood's grave. The cemetery is behind a movie theater in Brentwood.

DIARY OF A MASOCHIST

Remember when you pissed on me in San Francisco? You waited at the bottom of the stairs; it was dark. I came down the stairs and you crouched there, leaped on me, hit me, tried to stick it in me. C was upstairs. You pissed on me, I turned over and tried to absorb the piss. C had been scared you'd destroy her work, ruin her films. Don't worry, I said defending you, he wouldn't do that.

In Phoenix you said I was Kissinger because I couldn't explain a line in H's story. 'I was eight when I had my first affair.' You told me you tried to put your hand on your aunt's cunt when you were five. I didn't call you Tricky Dick for that. Kept me up all night long in a Phoenix motel room, calling me Nixon, all night long, TV on, your eyes holes in your head. I made phone calls my invisible thread for sanity.

Back at the beginning – but there's no way to compare beginnings and middles and ends – in Amsterdam you put your cock in my hand and said my cock is yours. You had been my friend for three years. You held me all the way to NYC, and our first night fucking, worried that my sister would hear us. I thought that was strange but already I was gone and thought if you were concerned, probably you were just more sensitive.

In Buffalo you get the flu. Your hands turn red, you cry and want to go back to Holland. I nurse you; in the morning you tell me my breath stinks – I am eating less and less.

I dream two men are watching us as we lie in bed. I go up to them (they are very tall, I am barefoot) and demand that they stop. I tell you my dream and you say they were in the room and you saw them too.

You warn me against S in Pittsburgh. I dream about your wife and how I'll be isolated again in Amsterdam. I run the bath in the dream and it overflows. I swim in its pool to turn off the faucets and my mother is angry with me for making love with 'a married man.'

We are not making love. That's what you decreed in West Lafayette, Indiana. There we are at Purdue University, showing films to cheerleaders, and in the Purdue Guest House you tell me you don't want to make love with me because it deteriorates our relationship. We show the films, eat Chinese food, you can't understand why I'm upset.

I sleep alone but every night you get into bed with me, then leave again. In the morning you beckon me to you and kiss me. The phone rings. You say I'm glad because we were being drawn in again. I want to go, you can do the trip alone I say. You say you'd blame me and so would everyone else. Next day you act ok, the day after, it's murder again.

We get to Minneapolis. A Hyatt Hotel. I write in my diary that I can't resist my desire for your tongue on my cunt. As I undress in the hotel, thinking about you and sex, I look out the window and notice a man on the sidewalk, beating off, watching me.

We change hotels. You say you've been keeping yourself from me frantically. You don't want to come, don't know what to do with the feeling. You want me to come — you start me, you stop me. You piss on the floor in your sleep. I tell you in the morning and say I'm not angry. Your wife would've been you say.

You wake me in the middle of the night and stand at the foot of the bed and say I feel I am eating myself up.

You are eating me and biting me so hard my skin turns blue and red. You bite me on the cunt and I ask you to stop. You say it hurts you more than it does me. I look at my shoulders after one of our sessions and think, the stain of you lasts so long.

The bus ride to Omaha with Chicago blacks. One calls himself a professional fucker and puts his hand on my thigh. We change buses in Omaha, get a bus all to ourselves. I'm ready to fuck you in the toilet, going Greyhound. You say your wife would be shocked. We don't.

Get to Cheyenne. I buy boys' cowboy boots. We play pool and some man promises me a silver dollar. A whore tells me there are two ladies rooms, a nice one and a nasty one. She asks, 'Which do you want?' We both laugh, we're in the shit together.

You say you don't like my body, but you like making love with me because I'm more skilled, more exciting than your wife. I dream a man who is crippled tries to lure me to his floor #9, and I want to get out at #4. Somehow I'm forced to glide past him.

In Boulder we meet B, the filmmaker. You tell him he's afraid to die. B says he made his wife choose making art or marrying him. B kisses me on the forehead. Feels like the seal of approval and the kiss of death. I dream four babies are placed in a plastic box as a work of art.

In Boulder we come and fight. Our host hates me, thinks I persecute you, until the last night when he sees. He apologizes to me and I defend you. I understand you I say to our host.

On our way to San Francisco. Fifteen hours to Salt Lake City where we register as man and wife. You tell me again never to have any expectations, any needs. We're in the Palace Motel.

On to Reno. I read, 'but also all journeys have secret destinations of which the traveler is unaware.' You write a letter to your wife. I ask why you're so much clearer now about the situation with your wife. You say because you are with me now. You say you're not turned on by me.

San Francisco. C's house. I dream about prostitutes and in the dream you say it's better to be a prostitute and not married. C and I are not married. You hate C and try to turn me against her. You tell me she's in love with me and can't love me. C tries to put up with you. You go mad; she screams at you but you're too gone and I'm scared, everything's collapsing. We see W's films and you tell him one side of the screen is brighter than the other. It's such a crazy thing to say, I wonder if you're right. This is the night you pissed on me. In the morning you tell me you knew what you were doing. C tries to help me and says you're going crazy. I can't admit it to myself. She takes us to the bus and we go to Portland.

We make love in Portland. Over Chinese food you talk about your wife, your kids. We are interviewed about film for a radio program. You tell me you were C's victim. The next morning I tell you how my father hurt me and you say you'll never betray me. There's money just for one of us to do the show in NYC, to fly there and back, and besides, you're scared to death of flying. The morning I'm to go, I awaken in your arms and we begin to make love. Your cock was hard on my ass. You enter me from the back, the front, then pull out. Let's have some tea instead you say. I cry and you accuse me of trying to make you feel guilty.

I do the show like a champ. Two days in NYC alone. Am down fifteen pounds and I can't sleep or stop talking. I show G and S 8mm films of our trip. The hotels, the bath water, you lying asleep in bed, views out windows to streets, an American flag, endless miles of America from a bus window, C, desert, mountains, bathrooms, lamps, snow, room after room.

Your wife phones me from Holland. I fly to Vancouver; you meet me and do not look at me. I ask you to return to your wife. I try to ignore you. We argue in front of our host again. Our host asks us to stop. We stop and you ask me what I want to drink. 'Surprise me,' I suggest, smiling. You say you don't think you can.

There is a party. Everyone seems so normal. I cower and when I dance see you watching me. You say only your wife can dance well. You say I should seduce my

partner. You watch everything. We leave the party and
in a French restaurant become friends again, get high
together, go back to the party and fall asleep in the midst
of it. Your cock is again hard at my back and I don't
move. I feel nothing. You ask if I'm comfortable and I
lie, 'Yes – and you?' You say it's none of my business.

The Dutch are supposed to be good at business. You
put my hand on your hard cock and thank me for the
birthday present I gave you, a fish, a jade fish. It is the
end of March. We're tourists in Vancouver and taken
places. Sadomasochism feels out of place in this young
dusty town, only seventy-five years old. Drunk Indians
fall out saloon doors into our path as we walk at night.
Our hostess is pregnant.

I write to J who should have been on this trip – 'each
day a dream flies out the window.' You read the card
and question me three times. I refuse to explain. I know
you will take your revenge when I'm weaker.

On the bus again, going to Los Angeles where I've never
wanted to go, you start the day by asking me why are you
more hysterical? You're afraid I'm cracking up because
I use my hands and gesture more. I ask that you leave
me alone. You imitate my movements.

Medford, Oregon, another fight. This time you say I'm
claiming you by writing in my diary. The letters I once
wrote you are fraying in your pocket as we eat dinner
and you insist I stop writing. I keep notes of our film
shows. You tell me you don't need notes, that you'll
remember. After dinner I vomit; an enormous shrimp
salad, the portions are so big in America. A friendly
waitress with a ribbon in her hair served us drinks while
we fought.

Before we board the bus to LA, you say, let's be friends.
You throw your arm around me and I think about
Amsterdam, before all of this, and can't believe that
fucking can breed such bad results.

C meets me at the San Francisco station on our rest
stop. I am still defending you. C is still my friend. F
comes with her to say goodbye. This time, as I board
the bus for LA, I feel I am voluntarily committing myself
to a concentration camp.

The first night in LA at the Hotel Cecil, a death camp
for the poor who live in the strip outside the wealthy.
We get a room with a bath and no stopper. A room
with numbers marked in black ink along the edge of
the doorframe. Cigarette holes in the carpet and a TV
chained to the ceiling. Here you try to fuck me again
and can't. It hurts you. You say we don't fit. I never
know if you mean physically or not and you won't
tell me. We fall asleep watching TV: a live wedding,
a prayer drama with Raymond Burr and a policeman
telling us about the latest criminals.

The next day we are picked up and taken away to
the hills, to E's house, to art, to lizards in the
backyard. I feel privileged, just out of the death camp,
then adjust quickly. The Governor lives down the road
from E's house and two secret service men are
always there. We sleep together in her house; I always
try to sleep alone, you always follow me. Sunday night
your cock is all bloody. You refuse to see a doctor. I
phone B and S in Amsterdam and see blood on the phone
booth wall. An uncircumcised cock sometimes has
that problem which is nameless in our litany. I have
no one to get information from and am shy about
asking W, a Dutchman in LA, to explain why

your cock is bloody. I taste blood in my
mouth.

More arguments with filmmakers about film. The East
Coast vs the West Coast. We play chess, you make me
play. I write long letters that I can't send; you send yours
to your wife. I wonder what E thinks, we're up all night.
I try to stop you from biting me on the cunt. Neither of
us wants to have orgasms now; and even with a bloody
cock, you still try to fuck me. You tell me over and
over how much you love me. You tell me you hate me
because I lack passion. You tell me my pain hurts you
more.

Finally we leave LA and are heading toward Texas to
stay with my other sister, the one I haven't seen in years.
I am nearly able to consider leaving you in Phoenix,
the morning after you called me Nixon and Kissinger.
Instead I try to exact promises of good behavior. The
motel we're in is on Van Buren Drive. I take a valium
and sleep on the floor. You put your hand on my cunt
and I push it away. You tell me you love me, that I'm a
fascist and you hate me.

Get to El Paso, midway to my sister's place; we stay
at the Hotel McCoy. I fall asleep but you keep waking me during the night. The next day, passing Fort
Stockton, a notice at a gas station reads, 'Dean and
the Fat Boys – Dance Tonight.' I write it down to enjoy
later.

My sister and her boyfriend meet us at the bus station.
They've come from a party and are in a good mood. We
have a beer with them and are taken to her home. You
and I sleep together again.

Back with a family, my niece and nephew, my sister, a cat and a dog. I sleep in my niece's room. You get the guest room with the TV, so that you can smoke and drink all night. The third night you drink a quart of vodka and tell my sister you're not attracted to me. You tell her she's your type. My sister walks out. Your wife and her sisters had the same lovers, at the same time. I talk to you some more, then give up. Wake my sister and cry. She thinks I'm crazy and you're drunk and mean.

I sleepwalk through the next day. You ask me if I want to talk about last night and I say no. I mean it. I have no choice. I have nothing to say. Later that night you talk to me about your wife, the film co-op. I listen and say things, then go to sleep in my niece's room. I avoid you.

The dog gets hit by a car. I see her go under the wheels. It's a disaster the whole family can share. The dog survives.

I don't want to leave my sister's house. Back on the bus with you, I know I don't stand a chance. Fifty-six hours to NYC. We're almost broke. Just one motel more. We stop in Atlanta. Pizza in the Underground. I push you away two times when you get into my bed drunk. The third time I let you enter me. The last time.

We get to NYC and stay at N's. I sleep near the door, on the floor. You get the couch. We have dinner at my sister's, where we began our trip, and you pick a fight with us about Joan Little's defense. You talk about it for two days. N gets upset watching us. One morning I phone KLM and make a reservation for you that night. You agree to go and we buy gifts for your family. I phone your wife and let her know you're coming. N takes us to the airport and after you're out of sight, I start laughing with her. Louder and louder. Can't cry. Now that you're out of my life, there's a weird hole as big as the La Brea Tarpits we saw together. I feel like one of those animals stuck there.

Days pass and I fly to Florida to see my parents. There's a message waiting from you: it says you've arrived safely. I get a bad sunburn and my parents buy me clothes. I fly back to NY with my mother's cousin who says my mother was always too much in love with my father. I have to go back to Holland and I'm scared to death. I imagine you apologizing to me and things going back to normal. I see a therapist who says I don't have to let you know when I'm arriving.

I land in Amsterdam and J meets me. The first time I see you we meet with M. You're cruel and M is shocked. He says he thought you'd never treat me like that. You phone me and call me Toots, say you don't understand what's wrong.

The last time I set eyes on you we do some film business together. I'm trying to get out clean. You drive me to S and B's and tell me you love me and that I don't understand. I look at you and ring my friends' doorbell and go inside.

One year later, I'm in NYC and you write me that you nearly killed yourself in a car crash and now you're even more beautiful. I don't believe you.

LIVING WITH CONTRADICTIONS

He didn't want to fight in any war and she didn't want to have a child. They had been living together for three years and still didn't have a way to refer to each other that didn't sound stupid, false, or antiquated. Language follows change and there wasn't any language to use.

Partners in a pairbonded situation; that sounded neutral. Of course living with someone isn't a neutral situation. Julie and Joe aren't cavedwellers. They don't live together as lovers or as husband and wife.

How long would this century be called modern or, even, post-modern? Perhaps relationships between people in the 14th century were more equitable, less fantastic. Not that Julie would've wanted to have been the miller's wife, or Joe the miller.

In other centuries, different relationships. Less presumption, less intimacy? Before capitalism, early capitalism, no capitalism, feudalism. Feudal relationships. I want one of those, Julie thought, something feudal. What would it be like not to have a contemporary mind?

Intimacy is something people used to talk about before commercials. Now there's nothing to say.

People are intimate with their analysts, if they're lucky. What could be more intimate than an advertisement for Ivory soap? It's impossible not to be affected.

The manufacture of desire and the evidence of real desire. But 'real' desire is for what – for what is real or manufactured?

Other people's passions always leave you cold. There is nothing like really being held. They didn't expect to be everything to each other.

The first year they lived together was a battle to be together and to be separate. A silent battle, because you can't fight the fight together, it defeats the purpose of the battle.

You can't talk about relationships, at least they didn't; they talked about things that happened and things that didn't. Daily life is very daily.

The great adventure, the pioneering thing, is to live together and not be a couple. The expectation is indefatigable and exhausting. Julie bought an Italian postcard, circa 1953, showing an ardent man and woman, locked in embrace. And looking at each other. Except that one of her eyes was roving out, the other in, and his eyes, looking at her, were crossed.

Like star-crossed lovers' eyes should be, she thought. She drew a triangle around their eyes, which made them still more distorted. People would ask 'Where's Joe?' as if there was something supposed to be attached to her. The attachment, my dear, isn't tangible, she wanted to say, but it is also physical.

New cars, new lovers. Sometimes she felt like Ma Kettle in a situation comedy, looked on from the outside. You're either on the inside looking out or the outside looking in. (Then there's the inside looking in, the outside looking out.)

Joe: We're old love.
Julie: We're familiar with each other.

Julie didn't mind except that she didn't have anyone new to talk about, the way her friends did. Consumerism in love. One friend told her that talking about the person you lived with was like airing your clean laundry in public.

Familiarity was, for her, better than romance. She'd been in love enough. Being in love is a fiction that lasts an hour and a half, feature-length, and then you're hungry again. Unromantic old love comforted her, like a room to read in.

Joe: You hooked up with me at the end of
          your hard-guy period.
Julie: How do you know?
Joe: I know.

So, Julie and Joe were just part of the great heterosexual capitalist family thrall, possessing each other. Contradictions make life finer. Ambivalence is just another word for love, becoming romantic about the unconscious.

Where does one find comfort, even constancy. To find it in an idea or in the flesh. We do incorporate ideas, after all.

You can accept the irrational over and again, you can renounce your feelings every day, but you're still a baby. An infant outside of reason, speaking reasonably about the unreasonable.

Calling love desire doesn't change the need. Julie couldn't abandon her desire for love. It was a pleasurable contradiction and it was against all reason.

HUNG UP

We were about to move. The next day, in fact. Which I think gives one some right to be deranged. I called my friend, the man I live with, to complain, or explain, I can't remember which. He said, 'Hello,' and after my first few sentences, there was silence. Then he hung up. I instantly called back. He said 'Hello,' I said his name, and asked what happened, and he hung up again. Perhaps I'd been too demanding in the first phone call. I dialed again and realized that I was shaking. It was cold because it was January. 'Hello,' I said, and even faster, he hung up.

I always carry dimes for times exactly like these. And no junkie on Ninth Street was more desperate than I as I stuck my hand in my bag for another one. 'Hello,' I asked, 'is there anything wrong?' No sooner than I'd said that, he hung up. Why was he doing this to me? I dialed again. This time I got angry. 'What do you think you're doing?' I demanded. He hung up. I could see that that approach just didn't work. I was beside myself. I decided to call one more time and then take a taxi to see him. To confront him. This time the answering machine was on. That was the last straw. Now I felt like I was standing beside myself. I left the phone and headed toward the avenue where I waved my arms or rather jerked them upward several times toward the sky, hailing nothing. I forgot about a taxi, and walked in the direction I should've gone – to work – I was already late.

He didn't want to move with me. I'd heard that signing a lease together, moving together, was a form of recommitment, a modern marriage of sorts. An apartment is more difficult to get than a marriage license. But if we broke up, where would he live? It wasn't reasonable. And who would get the apartment? Of course, this had nothing to do with reason. I had to calm down and believe that things might work out. There might be some other explanation. It didn't seem likely, though.

I walked past several phones, wondering if I should give it another shot. I passed another one, two, at the third, I thought, Yes, why not? I'd kind of resigned myself to the inevitable, wanted to be adult about it, and this phone booth was an old-fashioned one, enclosed. I wouldn't freeze to death, an injury to the insult. 'Hello,' I said, 'I'm calmer now.' He didn't say anything, but he didn't hang up. Obviously I'd hit the right approach. I continued in the same vein. I talked about the work that was being done on the place, our place, as if everything was all right. My voice sounded deeper than usual, probably the sound of resignation. 'Why don't we meet for lunch?' he asked. 'All right,' I said, 'that'd be fine.' I figured he wanted to talk to me about the break-up and his feelings. He certainly sounded blasé, considering.

We were to meet in front of a Greek luncheonette at four p.m. Three hours later I walked toward it and noticed him walking toward me. He can't wait, I thought. I set my expression to grave, to suit the occasion, and decided not to be the first one to speak. Let him bring it up, I thought, he wants it. As we entered the restaurant, he said, casually, 'Some crazy person kept calling me today.' Ah, I thought, that's how he talks about me, the me he's dissociating himself from. Or perhaps he's going to act just like a man and pretend it didn't happen. 'What do you mean?' I asked disingenuously. 'I'd pick up the phone and there'd be no one there.' 'No one there?' I asked. 'No, the phone kept ringing, I'd answer and there'd be no one there. Finally I put the answering machine on.' 'You didn't hear anything?' I asked. 'No,' he said. I drank a little tea and looked him straight in the eye. 'That crazy person was me,' I said. 'You?' he said. 'Yes. Whenever I called I'd hear you say "hello" and I'd say a few things and then you'd hang up.' He looked at me over his coffee cup. 'Didn't you ever consider that the phone might be broken?' 'No,' I said, 'I thought a lot of things but I never thought of that.' He lit a cigarette. 'Why would I hang up on you?' he asked. He said this in a kindly way, much the way that the psychiatrist examining Paul Bowles as to his fitness for the Army spoke. 'No one's going to hurt you,' he reassured Bowles, having already moved a pair of scissors out of Bowles' reach. Why, indeed, I thought. Why does anyone do anything?

On my behalf I'd like to say that I am capable of learning, and the next time something like that happens, I will immediately think that the phone is broken. And I'll go on to the next. Flexibility is one of the signs of mental health.

ABSENCE MAKES THE HEART

The woman said don't leave me, then walked into a ballroom, the kind that is easily imagined. He saw her, she who had been left, in a purple gown. Her dress froze in the space she inhabited and it seemed to him it was by this lack of movement that she projected a singular state. The wine, musicians, perfume, dancing men and women, and the breath of lovers coming in quick, hot, uneven spurts was a tableau of such familiarity, unoriginality, she did not need to look. Separate from the others, she seemed to him a duchy, defined by borders both real and imaginary. No doubt those borders were in dispute, and she chose to stand alone. He did not think of her as stateless, bodiless, unincorporated. Such metaphors might occur with the absence of others. There was such plenitude, so much given to the imagination.

Her hand touched a mouth whose very construction seemed to spell pleasure. What a mouth, he thought, a mouth to create hunger rather than satisfy it. His eyes lingered on the lips as if they too were eyes that could swallow his by their very reception. Her breasts rose and fell, and that she breathed, was alive, was to him a miracle. Such beauty could not be real. Her round breasts must be the mountains and valleys of that unimaginable state. Hadn't he once admitted that one could not imagine a mountainless valley, a linguistic impossibility. But she was flesh, and he was careful to conceive of her – her breasts, for instance – as possible. He thought, Unimaginable is not the state, not-yet-realized is better. He was drawn to her, as if drawn by her, her creation. She was a painting, a study in purple, she was a dangerous flower, she was a fountain bringing youth to those who drank her. He felt stupid, like a story that doesn't work.

It was a battle for her to think. It was pointless. She spoke to herself. I am the one who waits. I am the one who will be waited upon. I have the kiss that can change men's lives. I can awaken the dead. I can never die. I am empty. I am perfect. I am full. I am all things to all men. She shook her head violently. He watched everything. The shake of the head, a sign to him. A fire lit. Something was burning. He felt ill, he felt wonderful. She was sublime, and he wondered how words like that existed before her.

His approach across the floor was a dare, a move, as if the floor were a chessboard and he had made his opening. He approached and avoided, missing the hem of her dress by inches, causing her to move slightly, but just enough to let him know she could be moved. Her movement irritated him. When he looked back he saw that she had resumed her previous position. His irritation fled and fell into an unwanted past. Her position was irresistible and unknowable. He thought, If she turns out to be like pudding, sweet but thick, it will be easier to leave her.

Just then, as he was toying with flight, a woman hurried to her side. The woman cupped her hands to her mouth to speak words meant just for her. He imagined that someone had been slighted, her indifference to someone had been noted, or perhaps it was a practical matter. She had to leave in order to be ready for an early morning rendezvous. With a married man. An important figure in the government. The woman took her arm and the two walked out of the room, their shadows larger than life. Were her eyes full of tears? Was she that delicate, so easily hurt or affected, such an angel to feel for others. The crowded room emptied with her departure, and love that is despair led him to follow her, to find her.

Her father lay in state on a hospital bed. Nothing was attached to him anymore. His head was turned from her and frozen. Couldn't she give him life, she who loved him more than any man. His hand was ice. His ankles were swollen and purple like her dress. His eyes were fixed and dilated. He did not know she was there. This must be death. And as nothing is attached to you anymore, no tubes dripping colorless liquids, I must also become detached from your body. Now, what man will love me, and who will I be able to love.

He did not expect to arrive at this place, a hospital. He covered his mouth with a handkerchief, telling himself it was merely a precaution. Her purple dress disappeared down uninteresting white halls. The sterility hurt his eyes, yet he knew she would see his compassion, especially in this setting, and think well of a stranger so much in love with her as to appear in her hour of need. He would rescue her from grief, whatever it was, and she would be his.

Her face was ugly with crying, red eyes covered by eye-lids that were swollen. The corners of her mouth turned down, her beautiful mouth framed by sad parentheses. The color had run from her cheeks and in its place was none. She had aged, suddenly. If she had seen herself in a mirror, she might have imagined it was because she was unattached. She startled him. He was the mirror she could not look into to see herself.

Her transformation was temporary he reminded himself. He told her he had come, even though she didn't know him, because he loved her. Would love her forever. He recognized, he said, the absurdity of his approach, but having seen her and felt what he did, could the ridiculousness of feelings be a reason not to act on them. Weren't they all we had, inadequate as they were. He told her that he knew one day she would love him too. He told her he could soothe her pain.

I cannot compare death to words. Death is too great a contrast to life. And love is an invention, but death is not. I was not able to give my father life, though I am unchanging and eternal. And you too will die and blame me. Blame me for having been born. Or you will leave me before you die, saying I have hurt you, shortened your life. Taken your best years. I do not want to take your breath away.

With these words he determined to have her. It was true, her voice was not as mellifluous as he might have wished. But what man could believe her words, words meant, he was sure, only to test him. He had waited forever to meet a woman who might challenge him to appreciate the brevity of life. Her reluctance must be read as mystery, a deception from one whose own creation was exampled in the stories he loved.

She turned from him, racing down the hall, her dress swinging around her legs, jumping at her ankles. Don't leave me, he called. Don't leave me. She stopped abruptly and spoke to him from such a distance that he could not really see her face. And he could not hear what she said, her words strangled in a cry that seemed closer to a laugh. Don't leave me, I too said, then walked into the ballroom.

OTHER MOVIES

Along Tenth Street, it's pretty quiet. The beginning
of the night and the taxi people opposite my building
have four limos out front waiting, probably, to drive
to the airport, but no one's gunning his engine. The
motorcycle club is out of town, the ten bikes that are
usually parked next to each other and which take up
one and a half car lengths, they're probably rolling
along a highway somewhere, or they've pulled over
to the side of the road and the bikers are drinking
beer and listening to the radio, something I know
about from road movies like *Two Lane Blacktop* or
Easy Rider.

Roberta's walking her dogs. She's got three of them,
two very small poodles and one big mutt. At first I
couldn't stand Roberta. Along with her dogs, she owns
three cars, all of them in bad shape, and she moves
them daily. In this way she participates in a major
block activity, car parking. There are people who sit in
each other's cars, or move them, or just look after them.
Roberta spends about three hours every day waiting for
the time one of her cars will be legal in the spot it's in.
Alternate side of the street parking means nothing to
you unless you have a car in the city. Then, if you

don't have the money to park your car in a garage, it controls part of your day.

As I say, I took an instant dislike to Roberta, because she raced her engine, turning it over and over late at night under my window, and because of the way she looked. She has a huge mass of dyed black hair, eyebrows tweezed into startled half moons, and she wears sausage tight pants stretched over a big stomach and ass. But by now we've taken to saying good morning to each other and she doesn't look so bad to me anymore and I guess she's all right. She probably never suspected that I had put a desperate and angry typed note on her car window saying I'd report her for noise pollution if she continued racing her engine at two a.m.

That was a while ago, around the time Richie got put away. Now he's down the block, drinking coffee from a styrofoam container, not worried that those containers cause cancer, just calmly looking at the setting sun. Richie's out of the hospital again and on lithium. The new people on the block didn't know about him then, didn't know that his screams weren't serious, and he probably woke them the way he wakes everybody at first. You learn not to pay attention. You learn to distinguish his shouting from anonymous and dangerous screams or from calls for help and you fall back to sleep. But these new tenants called emergency and Richie disappeared again. It took weeks to find out where he'd gone. Jeff, who's been on the block longer than almost anyone, hung a sign in his storefront window and many along the street, on telephone poles. WHERE'S RICHIE? The signs lined the block. We all missed him. Maybe Jeff's lover Juan didn't, but I never talk to him, he's very unfriendly.

Richie usually stands in front of the door where he sleeps. The rock group gives him a bed and food. He stays outside during the day, rain or shine. When Richie's in one of his moods, having a psychotic episode, he walks back and forth and shouts: 'Where's the Sixties?' 'Where's Central Park?' 'Who killed Kennedy?' Sometimes he just howls like a wolf. When he comes out of it, he washes and combs his hair, cleans himself up, smiles at you and says, 'Hi, how are you.' Makes small talk. If you can make small talk, that means you're well. One time I dreamt he was my boyfriend. Maybe because he's so steady in his own particular way.

It takes time to discern behavior different from your own. When I first moved in, I called the police because there were strange and loud noises on the street. I thought someone needed help. A cop said: 'You'll learn to tell when they're funnin' and when they're serious.' I think the neighbors below me used to beat each other up. A tall, thin black woman, a tough blonde white woman, and the black woman's adolescent daughter. Sometimes I'd run out my door and stand in front of theirs, ready to knock loud. But I never did. Two years later I saw the blonde go into an Alcoholics Anonymous meeting on St Marks Place. There's always a big mob of people outside just before and after the meetings. 'A good place to meet men,' I heard one woman say to another as I strolled past. The fights downstairs have stopped. We've exchanged names – Mary, Jan, and Aisha – and now we complain together about the landlord and the super. I like the women, there are always wonderful cooking smells coming from their apartment. Their daughter seems ok, but it's hard to tell how kids will turn out. Maybe in the midst of those fights, the little girl cowered in her room, on her bed, or was protected by an imaginary friend. Rescued by someone like Sigourney Weaver, in *Aliens*, who kind of looks like her mother.

Not so long ago, Telly Savalas was filming here. The dealers down the end of the street yelled to him, 'Hey, Kojak, how's it going, man?' Savalas gives the Hi Five sign, and the guys are content, even proud to be, if only for a second, part of the big picture. We're accustomed to our block being used as background, local color, for TV movies or features, even commercials. Cops and robbers. Drug busts. Hip and trendy scenes, the location for galleries, weird boutiques, that kind of thing.

If I were to make a movie of the block, one version could be based on *Blue Velvet*, titled something like 'Under Tenth Street' and starring Roberta as the Isabella Rossellini character, one of the rock and roll guys as the boyish voyeur, and Richie as Dennis Hopper. It might open with a shot of a large rat on a roof blinking its eyes at the camera and some country and western music playing on the soundtrack. The big city romance of the small town set in a big city.

Sandra might be from a small town in Utah. I see her about once a week. She could be the daughter of a farmer and his hardworking wife, long dead, Gothic American types carrying pitchforks. I figure Sandra escaped to the big city years and years ago. She's down on her luck, without a home and with a drinking problem.

Sandra's emaciated. Walking along the block, she's carrying two totebags and clutching a cardboard box to her thin chest. She heads for Susy, a punked out seventeen year old, and says 'I'm sixty-seven, can you give me a dollar?' Susy gives her a dollar, then counts her money to make sure she's got enough. As she counts her money, someone moves up on her. Susy shoves the money in her pocket and jumps in the other direction. The guy behind her, one of the rock and roll guys, is rushing and he shakes his head but doesn't look at Susy. He looks at Sandra.

When Sandra notices him, she asks for another dollar.

What I think happens to Sandra as she walks off the block, or set, is that she goes to the B&H for a bowl of soup. It costs $1.35 and comes with two slices of bread. Afterwards she'll reluctantly spend the night in a shelter where she'll have to hide her money because somebody might steal it. It's safer on the streets than in the shelter, but at her age it's too cold and she might freeze to death in her sleep. I don't know why, but Sandra has an inordinate fear of being buried alive. She keeps a notebook – she used to be an editor for a Condé Nast publication before she started hitting the bottle – which details her life on the street and her fears. After she dies of hypothermia or malnutrition, the notebook might be found and published in the *Sunday Times Magazine*.

Susy's about fifty years younger than Sandra. To me she looks a little like Rosanna Arquette in *Desperately Seeking Susan*, when the Arquette character dressed up to look like Madonna. After Susy pushes the wallet into her pocket, she looks again in the rock and roll guy's direction, needing a bed, or a fuck, a little love. Maybe she's a teenage runaway.

Susy enters a door near where the dealers hang out and where they, in gestures and movements as choreographed as any ballet, walk past each other or a client and exchange small plastic envelopes for money. Susy disappears behind a dark grey steel door. Behind this grey door the girl might be shooting up, doing her nails, abusing her child or talking to her mother on the phone. On the other hand she could be a lab technician. From across the street I follow her disappearance, the door an obstacle to my camera, not, of course, to my fantasy.

I think: Susy's in her room, or someone else's room, or in a hallway on the third floor. I try to picture her. I ask myself, what's she doing? If I could I'd follow Susy inside, and stand invisibly next to her, then maybe I'd rob her story, steal it away to look at and consider.

Recently I watched a TV program about a woman robber who did her breaking and entering in Hollywood in broad daylight. She said steel doors were practically impossible to get past but she could open anything else. She loved the thrill of being inside somebody else's house, knowing that at any moment the owner might walk in and that she might get caught. A variation on the primal scene, I suppose. Part of her punishment, in addition to going to jail, was to be videotaped teaching cops how to catch a smart thief like herself. She enjoyed telling what she knew to people she outsmarted more than four hundred times. She enjoyed being on camera, caught by it, performing for the cops, her captors. But like Susy's story the robber's story, even though documented, is hidden from view, blighted by incoherence and the impoverishment of explanation. Still, I can see her on the job. Maybe I'm another kind of thief with desires just as strong as those that compelled the Hollywood woman to break and enter in broad daylight and to want to get caught. I don't want to get caught.

Suppose Susy's caught up with a crowd, as in *River's Edge*, a crowd so alienated and detached they don't report the murder of a friend by a friend. Everyday they go and look at her body decaying. They watch her skin turn yellow and green, her lips dark purplish black. Perhaps Susy's the one who wants the movie's good guy to tell the police. Perhaps she's as fascinated with the rotting body as I am with her story. Or maybe she's more like the dance instructor in *Dirty Dancing* who needs to get an abortion because one of the young, rich patrons at the hotel where she works got her pregnant but he won't help her out. Now Susy's on

Tenth Street, a runaway carrying a baby she doesn't
want.

Watching her with me, I'm sure of this, is a man in
a wheelchair who lives on the ground floor behind a
plateglass window. He has as unrestricted a view of
the street as you can get. We never speak nor do we
say hello. I don't know his name, but I think of him
as Jimmy Stewart in *Rear Window*. Except for some
reason he's the predator, not the victim. It may be
that he's collecting their stories too and we're natural
competitors. He lives next door to the man with seven
dogs and ten cats. I know Jimmy Stewart watches Susy
because his wheelchair moves ever so slightly when she
walks down the block and he bends from the waist to
see her better. He seems sinister to me, his fascination
a little like mine. When I look in his plateglass window
I see him and a reflection of myself, in fact I'm just to
the left of myself.

Suppose Jimmy Stewart leads a secret life, is not
actually handicapped, is in fact a murderer, and has
his eye on Susy. Or on one of the rock and roll
guys, or on Roberta. Funny Roberta. She passes a
lot of time in front of Jimmy's window. Many of her
parking spots land up right in front of it. Or maybe
Jimmy's a Vietnam veteran who got shot in the legs.
Most likely he was at My Lai, that's where I see him.
His actions during that massacre live with him daily,
and he will never, never forget or get over them. Like
the machine he was supposed to become in training,
like the boys who become men in *Full Metal Jacket* by
learning to kill and then doing it to rock and roll songs
on the soundtrack of the movie, Jimmy Stewart was
transformed at My Lai into a human monster more
terrible than he could ever have dreamed or than could
ever be shown in horror movies. What was inside him
was as destructive and grotesque as what was around

him. His thoughts then. His thoughts now. Maybe he sees nothing when he looks out his window. Maybe it's all just a big blank. On the other hand, he reads the *New York Times* every day.

I pass by his window. He's gripping his head in his hands. Roberta's on the sidewalk struggling with her mutt and trying to clean up the shit from her two poodles. Richie's in a doorway three buildings from this scene, and he's humming a tune, which sounds like Sinatra's version of 'My Way.' Usually he sings Motown classics. This could turn into a musical comedy, with Richie, all cleaned up, a Marlon Brando-type hood in *Guys and Dolls*, or maybe Richie'd get the Sinatra role, Nathan Detroit, since he's singing one of his songs already. Roberta could be the heroine and work for the Salvation Army. Jimmy Stewart could be one of the guys, a third-rate mobster looking for a crap game. Better yet, it's *The Buddy Holly Story* and instead of Gary Busey as Buddy Holly, he's played by one of the rock and roll guys, with Richie, the acoustic bass player for the Crickets, and Jimmy Stewart as a record executive who wouldn't, of course, do any singing.

Actually, I don't think the man in the wheelchair would ever get cast for a part in a musical, rock or otherwise, not even *Pennies from Heaven*. He's a Bruce Dern type, a bitter man with a dark past. Or, as he's already in a wheelchair, he could be Raymond Burr in *Ironside*. Nothing like a courtroom and a trial for that intense excitement, drama and awe once found in the church or theater.

When the sun goes down, people either stay in and watch TV or go out. As I said, Sandra disappears. Richie stands in the doorway til pretty late in the evening, then wanders. The neighbors below me cook and listen to music. Larry and Martin, a couple who run the Thrift Shop on First Avenue, usually pick up Harvey, who has a bad heart, and take him to one of two hangouts, B and Seventh or Bar Beirut. Every neighborhood needs a couple of bars, every neighborhood movie or TV series needs a meeting place, where the richness and complexity of human life unfolds in a series of interlocking vignettes. The bar on Avenue B and Seventh is my choice since it's already been used for numerous Miller Beer ads as well as for Paul Newman in *The Verdict*.

Imagine the place. A corner building. Red and green glass windows on two walls of the bar, so that the light filters through in color and it's always dark, even in the afternoon. Pinball machines. A locked toilet that costs 25 cents to use, to keep the junkies out. A TV above the door. A horseshoe-shaped bar. The jukebox is good and loud, draft beers still cost a dollar. It's *Cheers* or *Archie's Place* except the ethnic groups are different. For the regulars, it's a home away from home.

Tonight at one end of the old horseshoe-shaped bar sits Harvey, unemployed salesman, a *Death of a Salesman* type, except I don't imagine he's had children. Just out of the hospital – another heart attack – Harvey hasn't stopped smoking or drinking. He's with Larry and Martin, and they're not fighting with him about it. Since AIDS hit the block – two young men died recently – and the city, so many people are sick, I don't see them arguing as much. Larry's got his arm around Martin's back. To me Larry looks like James Woods, especially in *Salvador*. Martin doesn't look like anybody. He waves to Susy when she walks in. No one waves to Roberta but me. Her cars must all be parked and the dogs walked. Now she can relax, drink a whiskey sour and shoot the breeze, if anyone will talk to her. Richie never comes in. He sometimes stands outside, like a watchdog, acting protective.

I take my place at the other end of the bar from
Harvey and watch him flirt with Kay, a relative new-
comer to the neighborhood. Larry and Martin are
talking animatedly to Susy. She certainly doesn't look
pregnant. I've heard that Kay's boyfriend took a walk,
a permanent one. Tonight she'll even put up with sad,
chubby Harvey.

Kay's wearing a cut-up T shirt with a Bruce Spring-
steen logo on the back. She reminds me of Sally
Fields. Her small breasts are encased in a pushup
bra. She likes wearing a pushup bra, to get a little cleavage. I watch Kay look at her breasts rest-
ing in their cups of cotton, silk and lace, then she
looks at Harvey. Tomorrow she's going to have a
mammogram because she's over thirty-five. One out
of ten American women, she tells him, gets breast
cancer. Then she drinks a shot of vodka and rolls
her blue eyes at him, as if she were Demi Moore
in *St Elmo's Fire*. They talk about disease. His heart.
Her breasts. AIDS. Kay's good friend Richard died
two months ago, and she still can't believe it. Life,
she tells Harvey, wasn't supposed to be like this. Kay
slides off the barstool, goes to the jukebox, and plays
'Born in the USA' and 'Girls Just Want to Have
Fun.'

Joe the bartender is nothing like Archie or Ted
Danson, the guy from *Cheers*. He's a tall black guy,
sort of like the lead in *The Brother from Another Planet*.
Joe lived in Harlem before moving down here. He's
friendly but cool, suggesting that when he works, he
works. He keeps his eyes on the couples and singles
around him. Sometimes I watch the scene through
his seasoned, professional eyes as they pan the bar,
scanning the crowd for trouble and requests for more
drinks. He doesn't betray much. He tells Larry and
Martin the rumor is that Edouardo, who lives two

houses from Susy, got caught dealing heroin, and he and his older cousin are in jail, probably at Rikers.

Edouardo's about eighteen, Hispanic, the oldest of seven children. Seven children from the same mother – she moved to New Jersey about when I moved in – and three different fathers. Their grandmother, who always looks tired and usually carries an open can of beer in a paperbag, lives with them and takes care of them. In their crowded apartment Edouardo – or Eddy – screams at his brothers and sisters, controls the TV set and leaves the lights on all night so that the youngest ones find it hard to sleep. On the block he plays the big man and struts his stuff, even holds doors for the 'ladies.' Then he laughs behind their backs. I wondered why I hadn't seen him around lately.

Standing outside the bar is his sixteen-year-old sister Maria. Months ago Maria and I were in the corner bodega, the one run by three Syrian brothers. A man walked in and in front of everybody started shouting at her: 'I'm your father. I don't want you on the streets. Comprendès? I'm your father.' As if we were watching television, a soap like *Dynasty* or a docudrama about a family in trouble, the Syrian grocer and I pretended not to hear, pretended to go about our business. When Maria left with the man who claimed to be her father, she didn't look at us, stood up tall, stretching her small frame, and projected a sullen dignity which I respect. Ahmed says to me, *Family Court.*

I'm pretty sure Maria is working the street. Tonight she could be dealing herself or dope. This is a crack and cocaine area, unlike Tenth Street which is primarily grass. Anyway she never comes into the bar, maybe because it's mostly white, then black, hardly ever Hispanic, or maybe it's because she respects certain traditions, like a girl doesn't go into bars alone. Maybe it's just that they won't let her in, she looks her age, or they know she's a hooker. I'm not sure. Edouardo used to come in sometimes. Both of them frequent Bar Beirut on First Avenue where the motorcycle crowd hangs out when they're in town.

Joe hands me a draft beer and says, conspiratorially, 'I couldn't see you living in the country. You're a real urban woman.' He's never said anything like that to me before, and since I'm there invisibly, a kind of Hitchcock walk on, I'm reluctant to become part of the action. Kay, who's never really talked to me before, overhears Joe's remark and, for reasons I'm not sure of, doesn't go back to her seat next to Harvey but sits down close to me. She does most of the talking and I realize she's flirting with Joe. They talk about real estate – what landlord has bought which building, which ones are being warehoused – and about the squatters on Ninth and C, the closest Manhattan comes to having a tent city for the homeless. It looks something like England's Greenham Common.

Kay orders a martini and Joe, to lighten the mood, says he's just heard on the news that martinis are the favourite drink of 11 percent of Americans. Kay says martinis make her think of Thirties movies, a different time. What about *Moonlighting*? Joe asks. Roberta takes a stool next to Kay and talks about a story she heard on the news. A pet psychologist refused to divulge the name of the golden retriever she was working with 'because of the confidentiality of the doctor/patient relationship.' Then Harvey, still chasing Kay, wanders over and pretends to be talking only to Joe about the porn he's been renting from the video store, the one that's also a dry cleaners, owned by Kim, the Korean who's got a lot of good selling ideas. That's the way Harvey puts it.

Highlights from the Iran/contra hearings play on the TV above the door and everyone but Joe turns to watch, listen and laugh. One old guy screams support for Ollie North. He's drunk, says Martin. But he's not alone, says Larry. Roberta switches from pets to vets and tells the story of her window washer, a Vietnam vet who said he wouldn't ever fight again unless they were landing on Concy Island. If I were really part of this movie, I'd ask who are 'they'? But I don't and instead think about the man in the wheelchair who never comes in here, but has been known to go to the pasta restaurant on Avenue A and sit in the window glowering.

Kay remarks that Freud once said Coney Island was the only place in the US that interested him. This gives Harvey a chance to talk to Kay again, and he says, 'You one of those Freudians?' She throws him a disgusted look. Now he realizes she'll never sleep with him. Martin and Larry probably are aware that Harvey, who gets very aggressive when he drinks, is about to lose it, having lost an opportunity with Kay, and they take Harv by the arm and lead him out the bar.

It's not such a hot night at Seventh and B. Kay says Bar Beirut is better on weekdays. She says she's just gotten a part in an independent film being shot in the neighborhood. The mood changes when Susy strolls by, her arm around another young woman. Joe, in an uncharacteristic gesture, takes out a teddy bear from behind the bar and hands it to her. Susy's friend looks angry as does Kay. It's all in close up: their anguished faces, Joe's mischievous grin, Susy's sense of her own power, her hands on her slim hips. Sets of eyes dart back and forth. It turns into a rock video, something like Michael Jackson's *Beat It*, and I see them all moving around the bar, snapping their fingers, taking positions and pulling knives out of their pockets. What's going to happen? I ask myself, wandering home. How's it going to end? Will Susy sleep with

Joe and desert her girlfriend? Or will Kay outstay Susy
and land him, if she really wants him?

I've often wondered what it would be like to shoot
a bar scene using as extras all those actors who work
as famous lookalikes. These characters could wander
back to the block, each to her or his own particular
place on it, with their own thoughts about the night
they've just had. If Susy were the dance instructor in
Dirty Dancing, and Joe turned into Patrick Swayze,
and Kay into Jennifer Grey, they'd dance out the bar
and into the street, exploding in an ecstasy of pelvic
thrusts and utopian feeling. The extras, of course,
would all join in. Or, as in *Hill Street Blues*, it could
end in a freeze frame with Susy opening her steel door,
while Kay and Joe kiss in the foreground.

I don't like endings. Besides, though the night has
drawn to a close, and is a natural ending, the next
day Tenth Street bustles again. Roberta's revving her
engine. Richie's upset and is shouting about Bush
and the CIA. The thrift shop has opened a little late,
because Martin's hungover. Jimmy Stewart's in the
window, staring. And Kay and Susy pass each other
on the street, but don't say hello. I decide that Susy did
sleep with Joe. When an ambulance pulls up next door,
its siren blasting, I run to the window, wondering who's
life might be in danger. Last week an apartment house
went up in flames, the fire engulfing and destroying
three floors within minutes. Everyone watched. Disas-
ters bring people together. I hope they're not taking
Richie away again.

THE TROUBLE WITH BEAUTY

'We may all of us well seek to close
our eyes to the scenes of our childhood.'
Freud, *The Interpretation of Dreams*

Beauty's father reluctantly left her alone with Beast.
He stumbled along the path that led home, turning
now and then to look back at Beauty, mournfully.
Beauty and her father waved to each other, and as
he got farther and farther down the long tree-lined
lane, she could see him less and less clearly. Finally,
he was just a tiny smudge on the horizon. Beauty
remembered that a friend of hers had once observed
that people did actually get smaller the farther they
were from you. Then her father was gone. He might,
she thought dramatically, die of a broken heart.

Beauty was hungry and tired. Despite the riches and
treasures around her, she didn't feel beautiful, but the
looking glass insisted she was. Beast had provided a
dining table covered with meats, fowl and an array of
delicacies, all for her. While eating, Beauty listened to
soothing songs, not unlike lullabies, played by wandering minstrels. And, as she fell asleep, Beauty pictured
her father at home, where, sitting in the living room

with her sisters and brothers, he was displaying the jewels and gold that Beast had paid for her in the bargain for her father's life.

In the daytime Beast's palace opened up to her and revealed its delights. The garden was filled with rare songbirds and tame, friendly animals. Inside, room after magnificent room disclosed secrets to keep Beauty entertained and happy. The windows not only gave forth on spectacular views but were also openings to stages on which a variety of drama and comedy was enacted for her pleasure. Her days were unsullied by the ordinary. Though alone and abruptly separated from her family, Beauty was in some odd way at peace in the palace. At night, when Beast visited her, he was familiar and gentle. He had been, Beauty sensed, in her dreams for a long time. Not quite as ugly, not quite as distinct, but a vague creature like him had visited her when she slept, some desperate creature whose very life depended upon her.

Thinking this her headache began, first with an aura that lit up the minute sky in front of her eyes, then with severe pain, a fierce beat inside her brain that she often heard. Beauty lay down on her bed and fell into a deep sleep.

She dreams she is overwhelmed by something in the darkness. It's a form, a shadow that hovers near her bed. No, no, she screams, don't. Don't. She struggles. She sees purple and red. The walls go red, bloody violent red, and she wakes up. Her headache is gone. Beauty is eager to begin her day and looks forward to seeing Beast.

Beast's face, if that's what it could be called, was so large and distorted that even partly covered, it was three times the size of a normal human one. His nose was like an anteater's and he was covered in dirty matted hair. His legs looked more like snakes than limbs – he had five – and supported a shapeless sack of a body. But somehow his appearance didn't bother Beauty. Her older sister always said she had the makings of a philosopher. So when in her next dream Beauty was warned sternly by a handsome prince's mother, 'Don't be deceived by appearances,' Beauty wasn't frightened. She was fascinated.

All this was disconcerting to Beast, as well as his mother who hovered nearby, unseen. Every night Beast dragged his shapeless hideous bulk through the palace to Beauty's dining room, to talk with her just as she finished her meal. If she were happy where she was, or at least amused and content, would she want to leave? Would she want to return to her family, so that Beast could wait and pine for her, nearly die and be revived at the last moment when she saw him, in another dream, gasping for breath, moaning for her quick return. It was to be, he knew, his felix culpa. But Beauty gave no sign of wanting to go home.

Beauty and Beast passed nights in idle conversation, if Beauty wasn't stricken with a headache. But on one such evening when Beast came to talk to her, the headache pounded so intensely, Beauty wasn't herself. That is, Beauty spoke with an old man's voice, a raw angry voice. And she cursed too, spitting out vile and salacious words that even Beast didn't know. Singing bawdy sea shanties, she was like a demented sailor. Beast shook her and Beauty fell into a sleep so deep Beast feared she might be dead. When she awoke, she was herself. Then, as usual, Beast asked her if she loved him and she said no.

Time passed and the putrid voice of the old man emerged from Beauty more often, during the night and sometimes during the day. Beast could hear it even from his faraway living quarters at the other side of the palace, and after conferring with his unhappy mother, it was Beast himself who proposed that Beauty might want a vacation, a visit with her beloved family. Beauty stared at him. He was incredibly, wonderfully ugly, moving across the floor like an overgrown insect. 'All right,' she answered. 'I'll go.' The Beast bellowed: 'If you love me, you'll marry me when you return. And if you don't return in due course, in two months, I will die.' Beauty stared at him again. Beast felt odder than ever, his speech so long in the offing, hollow, perhaps tinny, to his many ears. Everything depended on it.

So Beauty went home, transported swiftly on Beast's magic horse. Beast worried, for he knew Beauty didn't hear herself and didn't know when the horrible filthy voice took over. Though he loved her, her headaches had grown more severe and frequent. In fact they had grown in intensity along with his love.

Her sisters were glad to see her. Her brothers, too. And her father held her close. 'I've missed you so, Beauty,' he whispered, his unshaven face rough against her tender skin. She said she was very tired and went to her bed, where she fell asleep as soon as her head touched the pillow. But her sisters, in the room next door, were startled to hear inarticulate grunts and growls, the sound of a bitter argument and then profound silence, like the silence at the bottom of an abyss.

Beauty's dreams were the usual – a shadowy form hovering near her bed, an ambiguous shape reaching for her. But after two months, which passed so fast Beauty didn't know it, an image of Beast gasping for breath and moaning dire torments superimposed itself on the mysterious figure she was used to. Beast was lying on the ground, near the river, his snakelike appendages waving slowly about his hairy mass, rising into the air and reaching for her. 'Beauty, Beauty,' he moaned, 'save me. Come back.' 'Fuck, piss, suck my cock,' another voice hissed. A voice that got louder and louder. It was coming from Beauty. Then the raucous singing of dirty sea shanties that, this time, was so loud it woke the whole family, including Beauty's father. His normally red complexion colored to an angry purple. I'll put an end to this, he muttered, getting out of bed and hitching up his navy trousers in the dark.

And so Beauty went back to Beast and just in the nick of time, too, for she discovered him panting his last breath on the ground near the river just as she'd seen him in her dream. What a pathetic sight he made. Beauty agreed to marry him, for yes, she thought, if she knew what love was at all, she supposed she loved Beast and she told him so.

Before Beauty's eyes Beast was transformed into a magnificent young man, a prince. But he was not the man of her dreams, as he might have been for many girls. Her dreams were much too chaotic. Beauty was terribly sorry to see her old friend Beast go.

It was a magnificent wedding. Beauty and the Prince were married in a stately chapel whose high glass ceiling reached to the skies. After the ceremony the Prince, his mother, the Queen, and Beauty greeted their many guests and dined with them at tables that groaned under the weight of royal abundance. Beauty was the most perfect bride the guests had ever seen.

After rounds of toasts and multitudes of wishes for a good life blessed with many children, at which Beauty felt the headache beat once more, it was at last the moment for the couple to take their leave, to race away under the full moon whose light created a swath through the darkness. The Prince gathered Beauty to him and led her to the carriage. Inside the coach, he placed a gentle hand on her sweet breast that heaved virginally under a white silk bridal gown. 'Don't,' she cried, 'don't touch me.' The Prince was dumbfounded.

Beauty stared at him intently. He pulled her to him. A string of curses in a voice as old as the sea itself erupted from her splendid lips which contorted into grimaces that spoiled the night and made the moon turn its light elsewhere.

In the fullness of time, as he delicately phrased it, and with the help of professionals, men in starched white coats who traipsed in and out of their bedroom, the Prince learned that Beauty had been molested by her father from the age of nine until he had delivered her to Beast. Beauty herself was unaware of this, as well as of the other self who lived under her lovely skin. The Prince, of course, had much to thank Beauty for. And he was never ungrateful. He had his own body back, he was his old self, and was more than willing to put up with Beauty. For, as the Prince said to his mother, the Queen, on a splendid morning that beheld the dawn of his own sudden enlightenment, 'It's not surprising, not surprising at all, really, to discover that Beauty is schizophrenic.'

A NOMADIC EVENT IN THE BODY

Dr Rene Richards, the transsexual tennis player and surgeon who was not allowed to switch in tennis so as to compete as a woman, was interviewed on late night television.

As part of her narrative, Rene Richards explained that when she was still a man she fathered a child, a son. After his operation, sensitive to her son's needs, she acted as both father and mother to him. She made him dinner, but also took him to ball games. She was his pal.

The interviewer, fascinated, leans forward on his chair, and asks, But what does your son call you?

Touching the pearls around her neck, Rene Richards smiles and says, He calls me Daddy.

AKA MERGATROYDE

When I was first asked to write about my family, the Mergatroydes, I thought I'd disguise them, make them characters in a story. Revealing your family is a little like revealing yourself. I mean, even my best friends haven't met my mother. Then I thought, make it hard for yourself. Tell the truth. I don't mean the real or only truth. Only network news has the gall to say what they're doing is telling the truth ('We're here to tell you the truth' – Eyewitness News). But I've decided to write as myself, Patricia Mergatroyde, only child of a wealthy and somewhat infamous father, Mark, the stockbroker cum jockey Mergatroyde, and mother, Marilyn Miller Mergatroyde, an exshowgirl who has spent her life living that down. And why do I even mention it? I who have spent a good part of my writing life designing characters so unlike my family that people actually think my pen name, Lynne Tillman, is my real name. Frankly I have exhausted my own interest in disguise.

The earliest Mergatrodye, or known Mergatroyde, discovered when Stephen, the intellectual Mergatroyde, had the family tree done, was a master builder in Scotland. Our family had a violent beginning. As a fiction writer I'd like to make the analogy between the start of the world, the big bang theory, and the start of our family history. But in our case the big bang was the lethal hammer blow to the head executed by the master builder upon his apprentice. It appears that this early Mergatroyde felt ill-prepared to build a column modelled upon one standing in Rome. So he left for Rome for further study, and while he was away, his apprentice went ahead and built it. And right in front of that very column, the master builder in a jealous rage hit the precocious apprentice on the head with a hammer killing him instantly. The master builder was tried and hanged not far from the church. In the corners of the church, Rosslyn Chapel, are carved reliefs of their faces, including two of the master builder – one dead, one alive – one of the apprentice's mother crying, and one of the apprentice. That was in Scotland in the fifteenth century.

Though I'm fascinated by this bit of history, it's the modern-day Mergatroydes, my immediate family, and a few more distant relatives that I intend now to chronicle. And at this point I'm going to drop my first person voice and tell some stories, stories as I've heard them, or as I imagine they might have occurred based on information culled over the years, the way oral history is ordinarily carried, especially in families.

Scenes from the Lives of the Mergatroydes

Mark Mergatroyde liked to say he was a gambler at heart. And marrying Marilyn was taking a chance. Starting to ride was a chance. But then he loved competition, being in the heat of battle. And what's more he never felt anything less than proud of his winning spirit. There are winners and losers, his father told him, and Mark adjusted his life accordingly. The only game he couldn't win, he complained to his wife, was the death game. Though he'd put money into research, he knew he would probably die before DNA was sufficiently decoded so that life might be prolonged infinitely. He was anyway going to have himself frozen, and had made specific orders that no funeral be allowed, since one day he might be brought to life and if anyone else was smart enough to be around too, he didn't want to feel as if he were coming back from the dead. He said that would be socially awkward. Marilyn humored him and secretly wondered if that meant she couldn't have a death certificate made up and if she wouldn't ever be allowed to marry again. It would be just like him, she thought, to win even after death. Or after becoming an ice cube.

Wallace, the inventor Mergatroyde, was always jealous of his brother, Mark, the stockbroker, not only because he had taken the family money and multiplied it many times, but also because he was so successful in everything else. Wallace's inventions kept his family in clothes and college, but he had alienated the affections of his wife, Charlotte, his son, Michael, and his daughter, Greta. Greta's feelings for him would always be confused. Somewhere between revulsion and guilt, some of which he shared. Wallace kept having the same dream. He's twenty-two and Mark is twenty-five. Mark is traveling the wide world, on his honeymoon. Mark and Marilyn visit the Scottish church and send a postcard of the Apprentice's column. The Rosslyn Chapel, the card says, is one of Scotland's loveliest. The column looks something like Mark and Marilyn's wedding cake. Three bands of ornate decoration swirl around it, kind of like vines. The column behind it is bare of decoration. There is no spotlight on it. Just the way Wallace felt as best man, a shadow. Mark writes: Too bad you can't be here with us to see it too. Marilyn and I are having a wonderful time and want to thank you for your understanding. She especially appreciated your blessing on our union. We do hope you forgive us completely. Mark. Miraculously, as it is in dreams, Wallace is with them in the church. He takes a hammer, not a real hammer, but a hammer he might have invented, something that could also be a gun. He kills his brother in such a way as to appear as self-defense, and goes off with Marilyn, his true love. Wallace awakens from this dream slowly. His wife, Charlotte, wonders why he's in such a bad temper.

Greta Mergatroyde, the actress Mergatroyde, has just turned off the stove, stepped back from it, and stared at the grease on the burners. The camera moves in to a tight close-up. The cameraman, someone Greta can't stand, wants to pan from her face down her neck, to her breasts and then her ass. The director says he doesn't need it, he's got a lot of her breasts and her ass. The director tells Greta to project a strong will, a woman of determined mind who's vulnerable at the same time. She hasn't lost her femininity, is what he says to Greta. Greta takes a breath and imagines her father standing at the edge of her bed, naked. She says, Daddy, what are you doing here? She makes her face as stern as an eleven year old knows how. He retreats. But he returns. Greta conjures the scene, moving the muscles in her face, thinks she might cry, but doesn't. The director says perfect.

Greta's brother, Michael, the accountant Merga-troyde, had always wanted to travel like his Uncle Mark. Instead he took trips to the refrigerator. His family was at the dinner table. The nuclear family, except Michael changed the letters around in his head. The unclear family. Wallace berated him on having lost yet another job, and Charlotte complained about his cooking, since he had cooked and not his girlfriend Sally, which his mother considered would have been proper. Greta was tired from the shoot and avoided his eyes as well as her father's. She was unusually quiet, but Michael put that down to work. Sally, who had refused to marry him and would only live with him as something more than roommates, to the shame of his mother and hers, made steady, uninflected talk, especially to Wallace. He was always eager to explain an invention. Sally brought a big chocolate cake to the table. She could eat chocolate endlessly and not gain a pound. It was almost eerie, because, Charlotte would say, she moves so slowly with a metabolism like that. Sally set the milk down on the table, and since she hadn't put it in a pitcher, something Charlotte found unforgivable, Greta took hold of the carton and read aloud the name of a missing child. Viki Lynn Hoskinson. Greta said the thing that made her really sick was to think how they were probably all molested before they were killed. Charlotte told her to please shut up.

Harris Mergatroyde, the social worker Mergatroyde, was the person who thought up putting the pictures of missing kids on milk cartons. Harris was unmarried and childless. He was a poor relation Mergatroyde, one of the few of that branch of the family still located on the East Coast. The family assumed Harris' work for social causes came from his own sense of disadvantagement. He turned over in bed, nearly crushing the cat who trusted him so much. Last night's romance was still asleep and although Harris had a hard-on, he didn't grab the guy. He walked to the refrigerator and took out the milk and coffee beans, and was glad he didn't have children who could disappear. He thought, they were disappeared, a term used for political kidnapping and murder in Central and South America, a term used in a warlike or wartime situation.

Yet these children were disappeared too and if people didn't think America was at war, they were crazy. He looked at the picture of Rosslyn Chapel that Greta had taken two years ago, on her ironic journey home. She had called it an ironic journey. Harris had enlarged the picture of the Apprentice's column, and it hung over his bed. Ironically too, he thought, as he climbed back in bed, intending to get his money's worth.

Harris' sister, Laura Mergatroyde Williams, liked to smell her husband's underpants. It was something she started doing only after reading a story where the main character, a woman who didn't seem crazy or anything, did. She'd pick the dirty underpants off the floor where he always dropped them – just like her husband – raise them to her nose and breathe in deeply. That's how the writer phrased it. Then she'd throw them in the laundry basket, smiling. At first Laura felt strange breathing in deeply, but after a while it kind of made her day, having this little secret. God knows she needed a secret, to make her interesting or keep her interested. Laura turned on *General Hospital*. The kids would be coming home soon and the place was still a mess from last night. She hoped things would go easier tonight. Maybe he wouldn't be in such a bad mood. Harris said she could always divorce him if he tried to hit her again. There were a lot of single mothers these days. She still thought that Harris shouldn't have put those pictures of missing kids on milk cartons. She was going to tell him that it was sadistic to scare little kids like that. After all who is it anyway who reads the backs of milk cartons. When Laura phoned him, she angrily told him that only someone without children would do that. Harris said, So don't get divorced.

Mary Mergatroyde, the anthropologist Mergatroyde, had attended the wedding of Stephen Mergatroyde and Bette Bloomfield, the parents of Harris and Laura.

Stephen, the intellectual Mergatroyde, had encouraged Mary with her scholarly pursuits and she had a great deal of affection for her second cousins. Even at the age of fourteen, Mary had been interested in family rituals, like weddings, and kinship systems, getting a copy of the family tree from cousin Stephen. She wouldn't have called it kinship systems then. In Tswana, she typed, the words for money and rain are the same. The group before which she would deliver this paper was very different from her family. The extended family consisted of members she had only heard about – the Paris Mergatroydes. The Hell's Angel Mergatroyde. The Spanish Mergatroydes of New Mexico. The black Mergatroydes of Alabama. A meeting of the clan would be so interesting. Mergatroydes scattered everywhere, not that most of them would come, they wouldn't. The immediate family itself had hardly come to her father's funeral. But Mary wouldn't scatter. She'd hang on to her name. Her father had played his final joke on her, putting it into his will that she'd get the house only after she got married. She'd thought about marrying one of Harris' lovers, but hadn't been able to go through with it. Her mother had been great about it, Mary's lesbianism. It turned out that mother and daughter had more in common than a daughter might ever expect.

Floyd Mergatroyde was disgusted. It wasn't the first ax murder he'd seen, but this one was really nasty. His family's eccentricities were nothing compared to Ed Gein's, who wore his mother's skin as a suit. The story behind that movie you like so much, *Psycho*, he told his niece Doris, who one day wanted to make films. Floyd's work, policeman in Dubuque, brought him in touch with lives that weren't the sort of thing you talked about at dinner. At least he didn't. And he didn't want to go to any dinners, either, even if it was a meeting of the Mergatroyde clan, planned by a distant relative from the rich side of the family, who called herself an anthropologist. Fucking grave diggers, Floyd muttered. He had enormous disdain for his upper middle class relatives and their little deviations. And even if his wife wanted to go to that clan meeting, he sure as hell wouldn't. But his wife had social aspirations and gave him hell every once in a while for preventing their kids from moving up in the world. He said in his best policeman-like voice, The only movement in this world is out, and don't you forget it.

Doris Mergatroyde was very excited when she received the invitation to the Mergatroyde family get-together, the first ever, and immediately phoned Mary, whom she'd never met, to ask if she could film the proceedings. Mary instantly thought of Birdwhistell films, and said why not. It might be very amusing. Doris was thinking more of Sam Fuller and Diane Arbus. She had to construct an overriding, if not overwhelming narrative in which the family could figure as characters. She didn't want it to be a documentary and it couldn't really be a fiction film, either. Doris also liked nature films, but didn't imagine that that kind of narrator's voice would be right for a film about human beings. She wanted a lot of attention paid to relatives meeting for the first time. Almost everyone there would have Mergatroyde as their last name, or second to last name. Maybe it'd be a docudrama. She could call it 'A Roomful of Mergatroydes.'

The clan met in a centrally located city, Cincinnati, at a large hotel that caters to conventions and the like. What distinguished this hotel were the elaborate columns, four of them, at its entrance. Harris, Greta, Mary and I entered the hotel, climbing its ten or so marble stairs, when Harris noticed that one of the columns had vines coiling around it. He turned to Mary and said, Which one of us is going to do it? We all laughed, of course, not being fortune tellers.

And as I was there — note the entry once more of my first person voice — let me report that this get-together free-for-all was one of the most thrilling and devastating experiences of my life. As a writer and as a person. A fight broke out between family members I'd never met before who turned out to have a long-standing feud. One of the men, Elvis Mergatroyde, a gem cutter, took out his gun and killed Matthew Mergatroyde, bank manager in a bank that had once refused Elvis' father a loan for his farm. And it went under. Anyway, that's what Floyd said, the only person there who remained calm. Although Harris recalls hearing Floyd's voice becoming quite strident at one point. When people were yelling and screaming 'Call the cops, call the cops,' Harris says Floyd shouted, 'But I am a cop.' Elvis Mergatroyde is trying to get a lighter sentence on the grounds that his crime was something like a crime of passion, as it happened in the family, where most murders do. Doris wants me to work all this into a script — she shot over two hours' worth before the shooting itself — because she thinks it would make an incredible, almost unbelievable film, what with so much weirdness and violence in one family. But, frankly I'm not certain I'd want to collaborate with a family member, given our history. Still it is a good story, and Harris, Greta (who naturally wants to star in it), and Mary are right behind us, and have encouraged even this little exposé, such as it is. As Mary succinctly puts it, Let's face it. The American family is no picnic. Why should the Mergatroydes be an exception?

WORDS WITHOUT PICTURES

A. Everything was going wrong. Suddenly I thought I didn't really love her. She poured the coffee in a determined way. She never read my thoughts but this time she laughed and said, 'All you can really love is the dog.' I poured too much dog food into the bowl and the dog appeared, larger than life.

B. When I saw her I wanted something. Her couch, the bracelet she wore. It was hot. I felt time slipping by, as if out of my hands, and my desire grew. I couldn't hold on to anything. She said, 'I'll give you whatever it is you want but then you won't want it. You like desiring things for the sake of it.' The look on her face was sure. 'Things have a life of their own,' I answered.

C. The woman, who was naked, looked like a figure from a seventeenth-century Japanese drawing. That she was naked made me think she might be from the north of Germany or further, perhaps Sweden. She stopped looking naked after I thought that. A thought something like 'Nudity is permissible in northern countries.' I didn't wonder why but turned instead to look at a man I thought of as 'the tourist.'

He was so well-prepared for travel that, even though
he too was naked, he wore a cap. He might play golf, I
imagined. My friend was looking angrily at the tourist
who, in his effort to capture the ocean, which is how
I figured he might put it to the folks back home, was
taking his picture too. He always said what everyone
who doesn't like having their picture taken says –
primitive people think their images are being stolen
– implying that he too felt like that. He was not like
that – primitive – about anything but photography,
although the only movies he liked were Westerns,
which he said were Wittgenstein's favorites, an odd
position for a primitive, I told him.

D. I don't care what I hear. It is what I don't hear,
what I can only intuit or imagine that disturbs me.
Imagination is a weak substitute for the truth, albeit
not even a substitute, a translation with meanings of
its own. How I discover what is really the case is by
gathering all the facts. Generally, what was said. Then
I place those facts – statements, bits of conversation
– under a magnifying glass. Not a real glass, one of
my own invention. I think about everything that I can
think about that may be attached to those facts. It's
simple. What is not said is as important as what is
said, we know this from psychoanalysis, the power of
the repressed. Someone's history must be mixed in to
what has been said or left unsaid. One reads between
the lived and the unlived. Intention cannot be judged
unless we see its fruit – action. The hardest cases of
all are those in which the people under glass think of
themselves as victims. For no matter what their actions
are they think they are being punished. And their best
defense is more defense.

E. Betrayed.

F. It had been a reckless night. For all of us. It was no use, bringing in the officials, even men on horseback. This isn't a movie at whose end we can all be saved. All we wanted was to allow the center to disappear, to become the background, or, in other words, last night itself. It is senseless to try to keep order when our purpose is to destroy the ground on which pictures appear.

G. One can never feed them enough. Last night I dreamt that instead of a front door to my house, there was a hole. I am hungry too. There are more of them and they may have weapons. I myself am disarmed.

H. Should the lines be drawn that would connect them, they would take shape in another dimension. From one point of view they are the background upon which objects rest. Rest? Do objects rest and upon what do they rest? Assumptions of their place in our, my, reality? Just connect the dotted lines. Their faces would overwhelm everything. I can't be certain of that. They might be like the sand, upon which the ocean rests when it has a mind to. The ocean doesn't have a mind; it doesn't mind. And, in addition, the ocean never rests. The ocean cannot be thought about.

I. It was in a hotel room in Los Angeles, a very seedy room where we had gone to seed. The TV was attached to the ceiling, the management fighting against theft. We wouldn't have taken it. It would have been too much trouble. No ladder, no hope, no desire. The only joke of the night was imagining a giraffe who could easily bite through the chain and carry the TV away, the chain and the TV like a necklace and a bauble around its long, irrelevant neck.

MADAME REALISM

Madame Realism had read that Paul Eluard had written: No one has divined the dramatic origin of teeth. She pictured her dentist, a serious man who insisted gravely that he alone had saved her mouth. The television was on. It had been on for hours. Years. It was smiling. It was there. TV on demand, a great freedom. Hadn't Burroughs said there was more freedom today than ever before? Wasn't that like saying things were more like today than they've ever been? Madame Realism heard the announcer, who didn't know he was on the air, say: 'Hello, victim.' Then ten seconds of nothing, a commercial, the news, and *The Mary Tyler Moore Show*.

She inhaled her cigarette fiercely, blowing the smoke out hard. The television interrupts itself: a man wearing diapers is running around parks, scaring little children. The media call him Diaperman. The smoke and her breath made a whooshing sound that she liked, so she did it again and again. When people phoned she blew right into the receiver, so that she sounded like she was panting. Smokers, she read in a business report, are less productive than nonsmokers, because they spend some of their work time staring into space as they inhale and exhale. She could have been biding her time or protecting it. All ideas are married.

He thought she breathed out so deeply to let people know she was there. Her face reminded him, he said, of a Japanese movie. She didn't feel like talking, the telephone demanded like an infant not yet weaned. Anything can be a transitional object. No one spoke of limits, they spoke of boundaries. And my boundaries shift, she thought, like ones do after a war when countries lose or gain depending upon having won or lost. Power has always determined right. Overheard: a young mother is teaching her son to share his toys. Then he will learn not to share his toys, the toys he really cares about. There are some things you can call your own, he will learn. Boundaries are achieved through battle.

Madame Realism was not interested in display. Men fighting in bars, their nostrils flaring and faces getting red; their noses filling with mucus and it dripping out as they fought over a pack of cigarettes, an insult, a woman. But who could understand men, or more, what they really wanted.

Dali's conception of sexual freedom, for instance, written in 1930. A man presenting his penis 'erect, complete, and magnificent plunged a girl into a tremendous and delicious confusion, but without the slightest protest. . .' 'It is,' he writes, 'one of the purest and most disinterested acts a man is capable of performing in our age of corruption and moral degradation.' She wondered if Diaperman felt that way. Just that day a beggar had walked past her. When he got close enough to smell him, she read what was written on his badge.

It said BE APPROPRIATE. We are like current events to each other. One doesn't have to know people well to be appropriate.

Madame Realism is at a dinner party surrounded by people, all of whom she knows, slightly. At the head of the table is a silent woman who eats rather slowly. She chooses a piece of silverware as if it were a weapon. But she does not attack her food.

One of the men is depressed; two of his former lovers are also at the dinner. He thinks he's Kierkegaard. One of his former lovers gives him attention, the other looks at him ironically, giving him trouble. A pall hangs over the table thick like stale bread. The silent woman thinks about death, the expected. Ghosts are dining with us. A young man, full of the literature that romanticizes his compulsion, drinks himself into stupid liberation. He has not yet discovered that the source of supposed fictions is the desire never to feel guilty.

The depressed man thinks about himself, and one of the women at the table he hasn't had. This saddens him even more. At the same time it excites him. Something to do – to live for – at the table. Wasn't desire for him at the heart of all his, well, creativity? He becomes lively and sardonic. Madame Realism watches his movements, listens to what he isn't saying, and waits. As he gets the other's attention, he appears to grow larger. His headache vanishes with her interest. He will realize that he hadn't had a headache at all. Indifferent to everyone but his object of the moment, upon whom he thrives from titillation, he blooms. Madame Realism sees him as a plant, a wilting plant that is being watered.

The television glowed, effused at her. Talk shows especially encapsulated America, puritan America. One has to be seen to be doing good. One has to be seen to be good. When he said a Japanese movie, she hadn't responded. Screens upon screens and within them. A face is like a screen when you think about the other, when you think about projection. A mirror is a screen and each time she looked into it, there was another screen test. How did she look today? What did she think today? Isn't it funny how something can have meaning and no meaning at the same time.

Madame Realism read from the *New York Times*: 'The Soviet Ambassador to Portugal had formally apologized for a statement issued by his embassy that called Mario Soares, the Socialist leader, a lunatic in need of prolonged psychiatric treatment. The embassy said the sentence should have read "these kinds of lies can only come from persons with a sick imagination, and these lies need prolonged analysis and adequate treatment." ' Clever people plot their lives with strategies not unlike those used by governments. We all do business. And our lies are in need of prolonged analysis and adequate treatment.

When the sun was out, it made patterns on the floor, caused by the bars on her windows. She liked the bars. She had designed them. Madame Realism sometimes liked things of her own design. Nature was not important to her; the sun made shadows that could be looked at and about which she could write. After all, doesn't she exist, like a shadow, in the interstices of argument?

Her nose bled for a minute or two. Having needs, being contained in a body, grounded her in the natural.

But even her period appeared with regularity much like a statement from the bank. Madame Realism lit another cigarette and breathed in so deeply her nose bled again. I must get this fixed, she thought, as if her nostrils had brakes. There is no way to compare anything. We must analyze our lies. There isn't even an absolute zero. What would be a perfect sentence?

A turn to another channel. The night was cold, but not because the moon wasn't out. The night was cold. She pulled her blanket around her. It's cold but it's not as cold as simple misunderstanding that turns out to run deep. And it's not as cold as certain facts: she didn't love him, or he her; hearts that have been used badly. Experience teaches not to trust experience. We're forced to be empiricists in bars.

She looked into the mirror. Were she to report that it was cracked, one might conjure it, or be depressed by a weak metaphor. The mirror is not cracked. And stories do not occur outside thought. Stories, in fact, are contained within thought. It's only a story really should read, it's a way to think. She turned over and stroked her cat, who refused to be held longer than thirty seconds. That was a record. She turned over and slept on her face. She wondered what it would do to her face but she slept that way anyway, just as she let her body go and didn't exercise, knowing what she was doing was not in her interest. She wasn't interested. It had come to that. She turned off the television.

MADAME REALISM'S
IMITATION OF LIFE

A cigarette hung from Madame Realism's lips, invitation to disaster, for with it there she noticed that few people came over to talk to her. Sometimes Madame Realism felt as if she just didn't exist. Maybe it was her imagination, but she put the cigarette out anyway, using the museum's floor because there were no ashtrays. Under the weight of this relatively new stigma, she hummed aloud, 'Another opening, another show,' and walked past everyone she knew, without looking at the art, heading for the ladies room. How easy it is to become a social outcast, she reflected, which made her want another cigarette as she approached a door with a sign on it. Like many of the bathroom signs around the city, this one proved difficult to read, and as Madame Realism felt that all signs were signs of the time, she wished she could have instantly known whether it was unisex or not, and was relieved to find inside small stuffed chairs and large full-length mirrors, a stage set from some previous time. This must be parody, she thought, sitting on the toilet, notebook in hand, and entered this in a large scrawl: IS PARODY A CONDITION OF AMBIVALENCE, WHERE DISDAIN AND NOSTALGIA MIX? AND JUST MIGHT BE THAT CRAZY THING CALLED LOVE?

DON'T FORGET TO WRITE ABOUT THE TIME I WENT INTO A BATHROOM AND IT TURNED OUT TO BE SOMEONE'S ARTWORK. ARTIST CAME RUNNING WHEN I FLUSHED TOI-LET. Madame Realism flushed the toilet and put her notebook away.

Standing in front of a full-length mirror, she was star-tled to see herself once again. It was always weird to see what she was inside of, her conduit, so to speak. Certainly Madame Realism tried to control her image and hoped to register as someone with a sense of style, even if that style was hers alone. Madame Realism feared seeming *au courant* in a desperate and hungry way, yet wanted to be of her time, not to deny its marks on her, something not true of persons called mentally ill, their faces and bodies stamped by their troubles, their clothes thrown together, signifying distress. One does not want to seem disturbed even in disturbing times. But who can really control how other people see you? Madame Realism grabbed her notebook: GUY AT PARTY SAID HE HAD FOUR FAKE TEETH IN FRONT. DOES THAT TURN YOU OFF? HE ASKED. OFF WHAT? I ANSWERED.

Two women rushed the mirror and smiled at Madame Realism whose reverie was interrupted as she quickly hid her notebook. 'Are you really Madame Realism?' one asked. 'Not really,' she answered, continuing to smile. 'Why, do I look like her?' All three women looked at themselves and each other in the mirror, and Madame Realism made a face she never made unless she was looking at herself in a mirror. Apart from the opposite image problem, Madame Realism silently noted the left side/right side dilemma that everyone had. All their faces lacked symmetry and it evidenced life's contradictoriness, even its betrayals.

Hadn't a friend with a baby recently told her that infants lie, or dissemble, almost from birth, pretending to be in pain when they simply want attention. Lying, Madame Realism's friend said, is obviously necessary for survival.

One of the women said, 'This isn't a good mirror,' and Madame Realism relaxed a little, the idea of a perfect mirror terrifying anyway, and besides she didn't like the way she looked just then. Still, she thought, if there is no inner life or self, and I'm not being conduited, this physical presence, this facade, might be all one really did have. This raised the image stakes immeasurably, making the peculiarity of her image to herself even more burdensome. On the other hand, it could be consoling to know that that empty feeling is not just a feeling. After Madame Realism left the room, one woman said, 'I think that is Madame Realism, but do you think a fictional statement can ever be true?'

Shaking her head from side to side, Madame Realism returned to the large space, so open that its transient inhabitants could lose themselves for a moment or two, and lie like babies. As if they'd never be found out. The test of a good friendship is the ability to keep secrets, she thought, and avoided walking near someone who might tell her one. In this room full of fellow co-conspirators – conspiracy is merely breathing together – suddenly Madame Realism wanted to flee.

Perhaps she'd been in town too long. Never wanting to outlive her welcome, Madame Realism every once in a while disappeared, without telling anyone, and returned some months later, reassured. For as much as she needed to leave, she needed to return. One produced the other, in a sense.

There are ways to leave without leaving, suggested a friend. A cultural sleight of hand might be to dress as a man, to become Sir Realism, for instance. Madame Realism told him she could never be Sir Realism, but that one time she attempted to dress as a man, for a costume party, and had bought a tuxedo and everything that went with it. But with the outfit on and her hair slicked back with gel the consistency of aspic, she'd transformed herself into just the kind of man she couldn't stand. Or that she'd never be attracted to.

That she could become that which repelled her shocked her in a way that only falling in love over and over again usually did. 'I was,' she told her friend, 'like a quotation from a work or book I hated.' Disguise in this instance uncovered more than it covered. 'What'd you end up wearing?' the friend asked. Madame Realism said she put on a long black velvet skirt, a black and white checked jacket from the Thirties, and tied a loose, floppy bow around the neck of the tuxedo shirt. She pretended to be a French or English governess from the Thirties. Everyone else was either in bondage outfits or in nineteenth-century gowns. She talked with a book editor whose face was entirely covered by a leather mask, except for his lips. She said she had a great time. Madame Realism's face clouded over. Maybe, she thought, I didn't look like a French governess from the Thirties.

The phrase 'life drawing' popped into her mind, almost like a cartoon, and Madame Realism complained to her friend that she had always been bad at it. Her people had been too big for the drawing paper, essential parts like heads or legs left off. 'Larger than life were they?' her friend teased. 'Yes, like a movie,' she smiled.

From art imitating life, to life imitating art, and here they were at art imitating art and life imitating life. But instead of Frankensteins and golems running around town, versions of Diane Keaton as Annie Hall. Or that man Madame Realism had seen near the Algonquin, dressed just like James Joyce as recorded by a famous photograph of the author taken in the Twenties. Imitation of life or art or both? Madame Realism sighed audibly. Perhaps imitation is the insincerest form of flattery.

Nothing ever worked the way it was supposed to, everything having unintended effects, and all you could do was get used to it. Like getting used to living in a world of knock-offs, she mused, and said goodbye to her friend, leaving the opening without ever having looked at what was on the walls. If asked she could say she had been temporarily blinded, and truly, as she walked along Broadway, staring in windows but not seeing anything, it was as if her provisional lie might be true. MADAME REALISM REVEALED AS A HOAX, she wrote in her notebook. Just a matter of survival she reassured herself.

Madame Realism's lie would be insignificant compared with Wendy Ann Devin's. For one brief moment, Wendy Ann Devin had been news in the *New York Times*. 'SOVIET GIRL' AN AMERICAN HOAX, the headline read. A certain Valeria Skvortsov, 14, a Soviet hockey player from Kiev, is really Wendy Ann Devin, 21, of Braintree, Massachusetts. Wendy/Valeria convinced residents of Brainerd, Minnesota, and other communities, that she was a well-known Soviet hockey player, whose father was a Soviet pilot. He had left her in the States, she said, to fend for herself. Wendy's real father turns out to be a Braintree, Massachusetts cop, said

Sergeant Ball, the detective assigned to the case. Sergeant Ball explains, 'Apparently she's got an obsession with hockey,' a quote that ends the story. Wendy had posed as at least five different Soviet hockey stars and had even crossed over to Canada where she got herself a Soviet visa, and in doing so nearly was deported from the US. Wendy Ann Devin, where are you now? And, who are you now? Madame Realism wondered. No charges had been filed against her, but she was urged to seek psychiatric help.

And what does her disguise reveal? To have portrayed herself as an abandoned and homeless Soviet girl? Perhaps a longing to un-state herself, maybe like the yearnings of would-be transsexuals who find themselves submerged in the wrong body. In Wendy Ann's case, the wrong body politic. Could this be the unconscious' attack on nationalism, that which binds body and psyche to place of birth? A *New York Post* story might have read: WENDY BETRAYS HER BIRTHRIGHT. NOT SINCE ESAU SOLD HIS BIRTHRIGHT TO JACOB. . .

Madame Realism walked home, lost in thought, interrupted only by people asking for money. She gave a quarter to the last one, a young man whose eyes met hers for a brief moment. She turned to watch him ask others, noticing how they, like she, avoided 'the homeless' in similar ways. Anything she thought about people who had no homes sounded as canned as a studio audience's laugh track or a recorded announcement over a PA. The word homeless itself naming, categorizing, and dismissing in one blow. And so unrepresentable were these people, that when Pat Harper impersonated one on TV, to get 'their' story across, it became the story of the newscaster who cried on television. PAT HARPER CRIES, Madame

Realism wrote in her notebook, followed by: IS THE UNREPRESENTED LIFE WORTH LIVING? And, NO TAXATION WITHOUT REPRESENTATION.

Inside her home, the one she could afford to leave and return to, voluntarily, every once in a while, she felt the evening unravel like a badly knit sweater. And soon it would be all gone, like Wendy Ann Devin, who had disappeared into thin air, along with the homeless and the people at the opening. Thin air. Madame Realism walked over to her window and looked up at the dark sky, the kind that in the country would be full of stars. But here just a few were visible, positioned economically, almost like asterisks or reminders. Madame Realism left the next day.

COMMITTED

An original screenplay

Committed is based on the life of Frances Farmer, a Hollywood movie star whose career began in the mid-1930s. A rebellious woman, a leftist, a member of the Group Theater, an alcoholic, by the mid-1940s Farmer was declared insane by the state and committed by her mother to a mental institution in Seattle, Washington. She spent about five years there, where she underwent shock treatment and, most likely, was given a partial lobotomy.

Mental hospital, corridor
Footsteps. Frances' entry into the institution. She is being led down the hospital corridor. She is in a straitjacket, two male attendants walk with her, one on either side of her.

Mental hospital, doctor's examination room
Frances is brought into the examination room by the two attendants. The doctor, a psychiatrist, a man in his late thirties, is waiting for her.

FRANCES   (*Notices his polka dot tie*) Polka dot. Polka dot.(*Resists being undressed by attendants*) You're just a polka dot to me.

Attendants take off the straitjacket and strip her of the dress she had been wearing when taken by them from her mother's home. They carry her to the examination table and put her on it.

DOCTOR   Now, we want to make sure you haven't brought anything in with you that you shouldn't have. So we're going to put your knees to your chest for a moment.

His body partly blocking the camera, the doctor sticks his finger up her rectum. Frances screams.

Cut to: interior of judge's chambers
The judge, Pearson, is talking with Dr Taylor.
Judge Pearson is a respectable, prim man in his fifties, the deacon of a Congregational Church.

JUDGE PEARSON   . . . four more years of Roosevelt.

DR TAYLOR   He can't live forever.

JUDGE PEARSON   Fellow-travellers are almost worse than the Reds themselves. Roosevelt bringing communism in through the front door. . . I want you to be the examining psychiatrist on the Farmer case and I don't want any psychoanalysts involved. None of that . . . talking cure nonsense. You and I have known each other a long while and I think I can trust you to handle the delicacy of this case.

DR TAYLOR   She's too much in the sun, eh?

JUDGE PEARSON   Precisely. Her mother is a god-fearing woman. A loyal American. She comes to my church almost every Sunday. A good woman, but she tends to be a little . . . flamboyant.

DR TAYLOR   Somewhat hysterical?

JUDGE PEARSON   Uhm. (*Nods*) I want the Farmer case handled carefully. And fast.

DR TAYLOR   When does it come up?

JUDGE PEARSON   Her sanity hearing is set for March 24th. As far as I am concerned, anyone who holds her crazy beliefs doesn't deserve the freedom we fought for.

DR TAYLOR   Don't worry. There won't be any problem. I can usually determine a person's sanity with three questions. . .

Cut to: interior, mental hospital
Frances is in a straitjacket, lying on a cot. An attendant stands silently in the doorway.

Cut to: interior of radio station
Frances' mother, Mrs Lillian Farmer, talking into microphone. Radio announcer in background.

MRS FARMER   Hello, America. This is Lillian Farmer. I want to speak particularly to the mothers of America. Your children are in danger. My daughter Frances is already in the hands of the communists and if I must sacrifice my daughter to communism, I hope other mothers save their daughters before they are turned into radicals in our schools. Because of radicals at the University of Washington, my daughter is being sent to atheist Russia. I tried to get her name struck from the contest. But to no avail. I am afraid that Frances will never come back if she goes there. And even if she does, she will be so swayed by Soviet propaganda that she will become a firm communist. This is a growing menace in America. Through subversion and trickery our young people are being seduced into anti-Americanism and atheism. We must protect our homes with our flag. Thank you.

Announcer to microphone. Mrs Farmer in background.

ANNOUNCER Thank you, Mrs Farmer. Not so long ago, the United States was host to the First International Congress on Mental Hygiene. Held in Washington, DC, with our President, Herbert Hoover, as honorary president, brought together with the full cooperation of our State Department, the Congress attracted to these shores over 3,000 mental health professionals: educators, psychiatrists, doctors of all kinds, psychoanalysts, and government officials from around the world. Over forty countries of the civilized world were represented, and tonight we would like to present, in the public interest, and under the aegis of the Washington State Mental Hygiene Society, the thoughts that represent the current trends in the mental hygiene field. The following statements are all direct quotations from the men who spoke at the conference. 'We are beginning to realize that the typhoid carrier and the smallpox patient are no more dangerous in the community than is the partly-well mentally disordered patient. It certainly requires no stretch of the imagination to visualize what mental hygiene, by increasing mental efficiency, can do also for those who are presumably without defect or maladjustment.' Said Emerson: 'Already we can see that a well-planned mental hygiene can purify social life, sweeten family life, and give valuable assistance in the fields of law, industry and education. We may be over-enthusiastic, yet mental health *is* the explanation of human progress, the hope of human happiness.' Dr John Shillady, also of the United States, responded directly to Emerson: 'The suffering caused by sickness, the consciousness of the uncertainty of life, and grief over untimely deaths,' he said, 'have ever been the foster mothers of sympathy, humility, pity and faith, the common factors in the development of human character. The elimination of the presence and fear of so much disease has already tended to weaken these emotions, and may have made man individualistic, overconfident, and careless in his moral as well as religious life.' Shillady suggested: 'To check the maturing of any of the fruits of a successful mental hygiene may be one of the duties of our mental hygiene societies.' As one of the Europeans put it, 'we have come to America, we scientists of Europe, on an educational tour, because America is the first land where mental hygiene found its right humus.' From Germany, Dr Gustav Kolb: 'The losses suffered by European manhood during the Great War left large and deplorable gaps in the ranks of precisely the most important age groups. There will be a much greater number of mentally abnormal people in

Europe, as those who survived were physically and mentally inferior.' Kolb warned: 'These abnormal people are the grains of sand . . .'

Cut to: exterior, mental hospital
Tracking shots of the exterior of the mental hospital, while the announcer continues speaking.

ANNOUNCER (*voiceover – cont.*)   . . . which may hinder or destroy the elaborate machinery of state and society. They are capable of changing the meaning of laws into nonsense, and the benevolent intention of social regulation into a scourge of mankind, and sometime they may give the impetus to the fall of Western civilization, which has been prophesied. We can no longer reject in advance, as we used to, the proposal to limit propagation of these unfortunates. To compensate for the future of peoples and humanity, we must seek to direct a form of mental hygiene which would strive particularly to further the propagation of mentally superior human beings.' Professor G.T. Ferrari of Italy: 'The movement has been preoccupied for a long time with young people who fell ill or who had become perverts. But the idea of taking care of youth in its entirety, even of those who are not ill and perhaps never will be, could be born only in North America, because of the freshness and the courage with which she faces facts and problems, and also because of her great riches.' Said Ferrari: 'Signor Mussolini, in governing Italy, has been able to give to the nation a habit of hierarchical discipline, annoying to adults, but about which youth are enthusiastic, and of which one cannot fail to recognize the great didactic values.'

Cut to: interior, mental hospital
Frances struggling silently on a cot.

Cut to: interior, Farmer house
It is Christmastime. Frances' mother is at the piano, playing 'Silent Night.' She is speaking aloud as she plays.

MRS FARMER   I did what I had to do. She was always wild. Smart, though, very smart, and I was so proud of her. I tried to give her everything I could, helped her get anything she wanted.

Cut to: interior of mother's bedroom
Lillian Farmer is alone in her bedroom. She finishes making the bed, banging the pillow with some unexpected anger. She smooths the bedspread, finds lint on her dress and compulsively picks it off. Then she sits down on the bed to put on her shoes. After they're on, she walks to the sewing machine and looks through her sewing basket, as if she's about to begin to work. Suddenly she stops, puts away her sewing, and rises from the chair. She walks back to the bed and sits down.

Cut to: hospital, exterior
Frances is speaking with a nurse on the stairs outside one of the hospital buildings. Long shot.

FRANCES   ... I won a crummy $100 and you'd have thought the world had caved in. 'What is becoming of our country when a young girl receives a $100 reward for celebrating the death of God?'

NURSE What did your parents do?

FRANCES My father wasn't around much. But my mother was proud that I'd won the prize. A minister denounced me in church and she leapt up and spoke for me. There was a terrific uproar. Of course I was mortified, sitting there in church with my mother yelling. I can't remember if my father was there or not. Probably he wasn't. They didn't really get along. . . Later, when I was in college, she divorced him. And when he tried to visit us, she took a few shots at him. . .

NURSE Your mother took a gun. . .?

FRANCES A shotgun. But there were only blanks in it. The two of them landed in jail. He didn't press charges. He used to threaten to put her away, and she'd say: 'Go ahead. If they certify me, I can kill you and get away with it.'

Cut to: backyard of Farmer house
Frances' mother is talking to herself as she weeds and walks around the garden.

MRS FARMER She could have had a great career. She used to call me and say, 'Mama, I want to please you.' Then she went off to Mexico to make some movie about workers for no money and she disgraced herself there with her drinking and pill-taking. I know she was unhappy. She wasn't living up to what she could have been. Even her agent said that. He said, 'Lillian, you've got quite a handful there. She could be the best, if she wanted to.' That's what he said. And I want her to be the best.

Cut to: courtroom

Frances had been arrested for drunk driving and was on probation. She was arrested again during this period for a barroom brawl, and as she had not paid all of her driving fine, she came up before a judge for sentencing. She enters the courtroom. Cellblock door shuts behind her. She walks to the bench. Music in.

JUDGE (*voiceover*) You were advised that if you took one drink of liquor. . .

JUDGE (*voiceover*). . . or failed to be a law-abiding citizen. . .

Frances looks unrepentant. The judge glares at her disapprovingly. Frances speaks but there's no sound.

JUDGE Have you reported to your probation officer as required?

Frances is close to the bench. Her lips mime speech but again there's no sound.

JUDGE Frances Farmer, I sentence you to one hundred and eighty days in jail.

Judge walks out of the courtroom. Frances yells in silence.

Cut to: exterior, mental hospital

Frances is speaking to the nurse. They are on the grounds of the mental hospital. The nurse is sitting on a bench. Frances is standing.

FRANCES Do you ever lie?

NURSE   Sometimes. You have to, sometimes.

FRANCES   I can't. If someone's a bastard, I tell them. Anyway, my acting teacher really had faith in me. She sponsored me to win a trip to Russia, and I won. The Soviet Union, Stanislavsky, the Moscow Art Theater. I wanted to go. It caused another furor in the press. The drama department was attacked for being a hotbed of communism.

NURSE   You and the press.

FRANCES   Funny that I wanted to be a journalist. Controversy followed me like a mad dog.

Cut to: interior, judge's office

JUDGE PEARSON   Now, her legal rights must be protected.

LAWYER   Of course.

JUDGE PEARSON   But she is a recidivist. (*Pause*) Well, I don't think I need go into her political background. It's well known that she has a history of supporting communist causes.

Cut to: interior, mental hospital
Bathroom. Frances and the nurse are talking. An attendant and another patient walk into a stall while Frances smokes and talks.

FRANCES   The judge was a leader of the American vigilantes of Washington.

NURSE   You weren't represented well by your lawyer, either.

FRANCES   I wasn't represented well at all. I wasn't represented, period.

NURSE   And now they think you're not well.

FRANCES   They've been saying that for years. I was framed.

Frances walks out of frame. She moves to the sink and throws water on her face.

FRANCES   Why do people think love is so damn wonderful? I hate love.

Cut to: interior of hotel room
Frances in bed, Clifford Odets sitting on a windowseat, talking and writing. It is morning.

ODETS   Where is there a law that if I write socially useful plays, I'm not a poet? Merely documentary. They think I've got no soul. What do they know? We had nothing. My father sold newspapers, my mother worked in a factory. I was a worker's son until I was twelve. Oh, I know what it means to be poor. Later things changed, but that was later, and already too late by then. And that's poetry. I know what it means to be on the outside, to be just a nothing existing on the edge of what America's supposed to be. The dream of it. How can you help wanting a piece of it. Now I'm a big success, and *Waiting for Lefty* is banned in Boston and New Haven. I know what success means. It's as good as yesterday's dinner. But you remember it. If I went to Hollywood... (*laughs*) I don't think I could go to Hollywood. No, theater is moral. Theater is real. I'm not going to get sucked in. And I'm not going to lose, to waste my strength. I want to be whole without money. I want to be whole without success. You don't know how easy you've had it.

FRANCES   You know, it really wasn't very different with us. We never had much money, and it was my mother, not my father...

ODETS   You're an American. You're as white as white can be. I am an immigrant. Now, we may believe the same things. We may want America to be different, we may want America to be better, but I don't even know if I'm an American.

FRANCES   I don't even know what that means to you.

ODETS   No. I don't think you ever will. It's like your behavior on stage. Now, in the Group Theater, there aren't supposed to be stars. However, when you go on stage, you shine like a star. You walk on stage like a star, and it detracts from the play....

FRANCES   In the Group Theater, the writer isn't supposed to be the star, either. Remember? The production is the star.

ODETS   You know, acting is a very whorish profession. You can say anything.

FRANCES   Acting is working. And writing is working. Writers can say anything, too. How can you set yourself up as a judge? I've worked very hard. . .

ODETS I don't want to hear about your purity, and I don't want to hear about your integrity. I'm sick of it. I've spent my life thinking about this. . . How to make theater useful. How to expose the conditions that turn us into animals, into beasts of burden. And you sashay in from Hollywood. I detest do-gooders.

FRANCES Clifford, we're supposed to be on the same side. I can't change my face or my background any more than you can. And I've been through hell and you know it. What do I have to do to prove myself to you?

ODETS You can't. Because you don't consider the conditions. . .

FRANCES I'm starting to consider the consequences. I'm considering what happens when your wife comes back from Europe. What happens to us then?

ODETS Let's leave my wife out of it. I don't want to talk about my wife. My wife is a saint.

FRANCES And what am I? A whore? A star? Your mother?

ODETS (*Reaching for her*) We're two of a kind, baby. I need you. Right now. (*Very softly*) I need you, and we're happy, right? It's over between her and me. Do we have to sign a contract like a couple of capitalists? Isn't love enough?

Cut to: interior of mental hospital.
In the ward. In the foreground, Frances is talking
with the nurse. Other patients are in the back-
ground, sitting, walking, painting with watercolors.
Music in.

FRANCES I didn't want to be a star. I wanted to act.
It all happened so quickly. The trip to Russia,
then New York, an agent, bingo, the jackpot,
Hollywood. I was twenty-one. Are your parents
still alive?

NURSE Both are, although one's been sick for a
while.

FRANCES Did they want you to be a nurse?

NURSE They worry that I won't get married.

FRANCES I was married. He joined the Group
Theater, too, but it was all over between us
by then. I think I was already in love with
Odets, but first I was in love with the Group.
We all lived and worked together on plays that
said something about our lives and the times.
Did you ever see *Waiting for Lefty?* (*Doesn't*
wait for answer, though nurse nods no) That
seems like a long time ago. The Group broke
up, the war started, the controversy among us
about Stalin. . . Hollywood never forgave me for
preferring the theater. After I played in *Golden*
Boy, I went back there. That's where the money
was. I was spending a lot of money on the Group
and political causes. The big boys punished me by
putting me in movies set in the South Seas. . .

NURSE   I saw the one where you wore the long black wig. . .

FRANCES   I starred on the cutting room floor. I was too difficult, they said, I didn't want to wear a sarong or talk like a kewpie doll. In New York, the Group was suspicious of me, but not my Hollywood money. And in Hollywood I was a snob for wanting to act in the theater. Everybody went to Hollywood later.

NURSE   Did you make any friends in the Group?

FRANCES   There were hardly any roles for women, so I was twice an outsider. I don't make friends easily anyway. They were hypocrites. Not all of them.

Cut to: dream/re-creation of last scene from Waiting for Lefty
(Male figure on stage, hands raised)

Cut to: theater audience
Audience yelling 'Strike' and applauding. Frances and Odets rise out of the audience. Frances smiles at Odets lovingly. He smiles and slowly (in slow motion) raises his hand and strikes her. Sound of very harsh slap.

Cut to: interior, mental hospital
Dayroom. Music in. Frances waking up in the hospital to find other patients standing near her, clapping their hands and stamping their feet in unison, as they listen to a radio program. Women return to their places, after attendant moves them away from Frances. Daily life in the hospital.
Camera tracks around the patients, ending in a long

shot. A dancing patient sits down on the couch with Frances.

PATIENT   I was a movie star, too.

Cut to: interior of mental hospital, conference room
Dr Taylor and Dr Kraus are talking about the Farmer case.

DR TAYLOR   In my estimation, she's a chronic un-
differentiated schizophrenic.

DR KRAUS   She has paranoid tendencies and delus-
ional ideations. And she refuses to accept her femi-
nine role.

DR TAYLOR   Unresolved penis envy which con-
tributes to the continued blame of her mother
. . .

DR KRAUS   Thus, resentment toward her role as a
woman in society.

DR TAYLOR   Well. . . I believe we're in agreement
as to the diagnosis.

Cut to: interior of mental hospital.
Auditorium. Tracking shot. Patients are watching a movie. Frances and the nurse are in the audience, talking softly. Tracking shot. Soundtrack of 1940s job-training movie plays in background.

MOVIE SOUNDTRACK   'I've got a job, I've got a job. . .
and it's just my first week out of school!'
'The morning mail should be opened and sorted.

Remember, never interrupt during dictation. The dictator may lose his train of thought. . .'

FRANCES It was bad enough that I was a communist – sympathetic to socialist causes. That was abnormal enough. Not only did I give migrant workers money, perish the thought, I went into the fields with them. I got my lily-white hands dirty. That meant I was really crazy. Trying to be visible. Shit.

Cut to: movie soundtrack

MOVIE SOUNDTRACK 'Miss Hayes, didn't you hear me buzzing you? Come into my office for dictation.'

Cut to: Frances

FRANCES When I got picked up for drunk driving, that was the last nail in my coffin. I called the cop a cocksucker. I've always hated cops.

Cut to: movie

MOVIE SOUNDTRACK 'Take a letter: Dear Mr Grant, I have several properties of the type in which you are interested.'
'Excuse me, Mr Harmon, did you say "type" or "types"?'

Cut to: Frances

FRANCES The newspapers crucified me. A female, a movie star who uses dirty words and drinks. My mother told the papers that I was preparing for a new role.

Cut to: movie

FRANCES (*voiceover*) They should never have put me in her care.

Cut to: Frances

FRANCES I shouldn't have hit the make-up lady. It was stupid.

PATIENT Shut up.

FRANCES Shut up? What are you? Crazy? Perhaps I've got a tragic flaw. Although how pride can account for my not being able to control anything, even my weight. . . . The studio supplied me with pills to curb my appetite. That may have curbed my appetite, but I think it unleashed something else.

Cut to: interior of the Farmer house
Frances and her mother are sitting on the front porch. The camera moves in on them in starts. As it gets to a medium-size close-up, Frances puts her head on her mother's shoulder. Her mother brusquely pushes her away and the two women continue to sit on the porch swing, which is moving, and to look straight ahead.

Cut to: interior, Frances' bedroom in Farmer house
Frances is lying on her bed. There are magazines on the floor and on her bed. She is listless, depressed. She thumbs through a few magazines. She cuts out a picture from one, then pins it on her wall. She loses interest and goes to her dressing table. She looks at herself in the mirror

and smokes a cigarette. She puts out the cigarette and with her back to the camera, she looks at a photograph that is framed on her wall.

Cut to: close up of photograph
It is an old-fashioned photograph of a woman in a hat with her back to the camera.

Cut back to: Frances
She is looking at the picture. The camera tracks back and she walks back to bed and lies on her stomach.

Cut to: interior of Farmer house, living room
It is night-time. Frances enters the living room to join her mother who is lying on the couch covered by a blanket. She makes herself comfortable on the other end of the couch and gets under the blanket too. Frances is going to show her mother pictures and slides of herself, movie star poses shot in Hollywood.

MRS FARMER   What have you got there?

FRANCES   Some pictures. I said I'd show you. . .

MRS FARMER   Move your feet a little, Frances. Give me some room.

FRANCES   (*continuing*). . . from when I played in *Golden Boy*. . .

MRS FARMER   Haven't you gotten over him yet?

FRANCES   (*trying to ignore her*). . . and from the play I did next. . .

MRS FARMER   I don't know why you didn't like that nice husband of yours. Your agent said he was devoted to you. . .

FRANCES   My agent doesn't know anything about my marriage. (*Turns on slide projector*)

Cut to: slide

MRS FARMER   (*voiceover*) You look very beautiful there, Frances.

FRANCES   (*voiceover*) Do you think so? They can make anybody look good.

Cut to:

MRS FARMER   No, really, Frances, you have always been beautiful, even when you were a baby. . .

FRANCES   All mothers say that. . .

MRS FARMER   No. No, you were special. That's why you should be working again. . .

FRANCES   Let's not get into that now. (*Changes slide*)

Cut to: slide

MRS FARMER   (*voiceover*) Did you wash the dishes?

FRANCES   (*voiceover*) What?

MRS FARMER   (*voiceover*) The dishes.

FRANCES   (*voiceover*) No.

Cut to:

MRS FARMER   Now Frances, you're supposed. . .

FRANCES   Don't make a federal case of it. I will.

(*Changes slide*)

MRS FARMER   (*responds to something in the picture*) I
liked you in *Come and Get It.*

FRANCES   Playing mother and daughter and the
same man in love with them. It was perverse.
But working with Hawks. . .

Cut to: slide

FRANCES   (*voiceover*) was the best experience I had in
Hollywood. It was too bad he was kicked off the picture and they brought Wyler in. He hated me. We
couldn't work together at all. We fought constantly.

Cut to:

MRS FARMER   You shouldn't fight with your director,
Frances. That's how you got a bad reputation. By
fighting.

FRANCES   You're the one who always told me to
fight for what I believed in, although you don't
like what I believe in.

MRS FARMER   You were such a good student, but that
acting teacher of yours in college was a bad influ-
ence. Communism, Frances, and going to Russia

when you knew I didn't want you to go. It was in all the papers. . .

FRANCES Are we going to get into that again? Haven't we discussed that enough? (*Changes slide*) Here, look at this.

MRS FARMER Who's that?

FRANCES One of the few people I could stomach in Hollywood.

MRS FARMER You were really alone out there. Too smart for most of them.

FRANCES Smart, yeah, but not smart enough. Obviously.

Cut to: slide

MRS FARMER (*voiceover*) Did you ever use that vacuum cleaner I sent you?

FRANCES (*voiceover*) Yeah, once or twice.

MRS FARMER (*voiceover*) That was good money.

Cut to:

FRANCES That was my money.

MRS FARMER Which movie was it you were in with Clark Gable?

FRANCES It never happened.

MRS FARMER   I hear he's a nice man.

FRANCES   Oh, mother.

Cut to: slide

MRS FARMER   (*voiceover*) You look nice there, dear.

FRANCES   (*voiceover*) I hadn't slept the night before. Make-up went crazy.

MRS FARMER   (*voiceover*) You shouldn't cause people trouble, Frances. It's not nice.

FRANCES   (*voiceover*) Mother, I'm not nice, don't you know that yet?

Cut to:

MRS FARMER   All my children are nice. You don't need to be so crude. You were brought up to be a lady. . .

FRANCES   Skip it. Forget it.

Cut to: slide

Cut to:

FRANCES   Daddy would've liked to have visited me in Hollywood, I bet.

MRS FARMER   He was impossible, Frances. He would only have made things more difficult. He couldn't have helped you the way I did.

FRANCES He was a nice man, Mother.

MRS FARMER But he was weak, very weak. Frances, I had to do everything to give us a position in this community. He could hardly even support us. . .

FRANCES He loved me.

MRS FARMER I loved you.

Frances changes slide.

Cut to: slide

MRS FARMER (*voiceover*) You don't know about men, Frances. Why, look at that. . . that Clifford . . .

Cut to:

MRS FARMER . . . Odets. You loved him too and look what he did to you.

FRANCES He did the same thing to all the women he loved.

Frances gets up and walks away.

MRS FARMER Where are you going?

FRANCES To wash the dishes.

Cut to: interior of a theater
Frances is onstage, in rehearsal for a new play that the Group is doing. Odets is in the audience.

FRANCES (*speaks line to other actor*) 'He came to me and helped me when nobody could. . .'

ODETS (*from audience*) What's your intention?

FRANCES I felt that she. . .

ODETS You felt what?

FRANCES I felt my character. . .

ODETS You don't know, do you? You come all the way from Hollywood for your integrity as an actress, but you can't act.

FRANCES Clifford, stop it.

ODETS You disgust me.

Frances leaves stage, crying.

Cut to: Frances' hotel hallway
Odets is knocking on her door.

ODETS Please let me in. I have to see you.

FRANCES (*voiceover*) Go away.

ODETS I didn't mean it.

FRANCES (*voiceover*) Drop dead.

ODETS You know that I love you.
(*No answer*)

ODETS I'll kill myself if you don't let me in.

Cut to:
Frances behind the door. She opens it. Odets enters her hotel room. He grabs her and kisses her. Frances tries to pull away; the camera tracks back in the vestibule.

FRANCES What do you think you're doing?

ODETS You're so beautiful.

FRANCES But I can't act, can I?

ODETS Baby, you know I didn't mean that.

FRANCES How could you do that to me? Humiliate me like that?

ODETS I am constantly humiliated by my feelings for you. I'm just a toy to you.

FRANCES Clifford, stop it.

Clifford kisses her, seductively. She starts to weaken. Her eyes close.

ODETS You like that, don't you? (*Still kissing her*)

FRANCES Yes. Yes.

ODETS You like that a lot, don't you? I am the only one who can do that to you. Aren't I?

FRANCES Yes, that's right.

ODETS You can trust me. Me. Not the others. No one understands you the way I do.

*More lovemaking. They lie on the floor. Frances is
breathing deeply. Odets pulls away.*

ODETS   Look at you. You're a monster.

FRANCES   Not this again.

ODETS   Say you're a monster.

FRANCES   We're all monsters.

ODETS   Say it.

FRANCES   I'm a monster.

Cut to: interior of Farmer house
*Frances and her mother are sitting in the living room,
reading and listening to the news on the radio.*

RADIO   (*voiceover*) 'Because tomorrow those soldiers
will get out of bed, square their shoulders, and
greet the day with a new Labor Day slogan on
their lips. American labor – producing for attack.
There's little domestic news of any importance tonight. However, in Washington there's a strongly
substantiated report in diplomatic circles that at
least four of the world's leading neutral nations
have rejected in principle President Roosevelt's
implied warning against giving asylum to war
guilty Axis leaders. Apparently these countries,
Argentina, Spain, Switzerland, and Sweden –
believe they should retain their sovereign right
in determining what individuals enter their borders from abroad. Turkey and Portugal are said
to share this view, and undoubtedly the Vatican
would maintain the same position. As a matter

of fact none of these countries have made any official reply to Mr Roosevelt's warning, but Sweden through her liberal press has already publicly endorsed Mr Roosevelt's stand and she will undoubtedly bar the entry of any Nazi warlord to her soil. . . Well, I saw them today, and there is a snappy outfit, believe me, as fine and alert a group of girls as America has ever seen. Sure, you guessed it, I'm talking about the Women's Army Corps, the WACs. Any woman who is an American citizen between twenty-one and twenty-four inclusive and has completed two years of high school and has no dependents. . .'

Mrs. Farmer gets up and changes the station to a dramatic program, then returns to the couch.

RADIO   (*voiceover*)
    Wife: 'This is an address on an envelope, some Mr Hatherby at Market Shepherd.'
    Husband: 'That's right.'
    Wife: 'I don't know who that is, if that's what you mean.'
    Husband: 'Oh, Mr Hatherby is the coroner of this district.'
    Wife: 'The coroner?'
    Husband: 'That's right.'
    Wife: 'Is there any reason why you should be writing letters to the coroner?'
    Husband: 'There will be. . . tomorrow morning. We have just been drinking poison, my love. Why do you drop your glass, darling?'
    Wife: 'I don't believe you.'
    Husband: 'This will interest you, Cynthia. You were a trained nurse, you see the poison was aconite, monk's shoot, home grown in our own

little garden. One-sixteenth of a grain has been a fatal dose.'

Wife: 'There's no telephone here. No car. Not even a neighbor.'

Husband: 'Exactly, my angel.'

Wife: 'Take your hands off me. Let me get up.'

Husband: 'No, my pet. In about five minutes, you see, the first symptoms will come on.'

Wife: 'Symptoms?'

Husband: 'Yes. Our throats will grow dry. Our eyes will turn dim and presently we'll lose the use of our limbs. There are convulsions before the end. But you won't feel them.'

Wife: 'Let me up.'

Husband: 'If you try to hit at me, angel, you'll upset that lamp, and, well, if you upset the lamp, this cottage will go up like tinder. We don't want to burn to death, do we?'

Wife: 'Irwin, why are you doing this?'

Husband: 'Why? Do you think old Papa Kraft is blind, my pet? If I can't have you, Cynthia, nobody else is going to have you.'

Wife: 'You mean Jim Craig?'

Husband: 'So it is Jim Craig.'

Wife: 'That was nothing. My tongue slipped.'

Husband: 'A cynic would say, my dear, that your foot slipped. Do you think I don't know what happened the other night at the schoolhouse? The Market Shepherd Schoolhouse at Lady Randolph's little concert in aid of the War Relief.'

Wife: 'Nothing happened. I swear it didn't.'

Husband: 'No? Then it was coincidence I suppose that you and that Dr Craig didn't arrive until the concert was nearly over.'

Wife: 'Yes. Yes, it was. We didn't go there together. We met in a little hall outside the auditorium. It was just as you were finishing your number on the accordion. . .'

Frances walks out of the living room. Mrs Farmer watches her.

Cut to: exterior of mental hospital
Silent. Frances is sitting on a bench on the hospital grounds, thinking.

Cut to: interior of Farmer house, kitchen
Frances and her mother are in the kitchen for breakfast. There is no speech for a while. Tension is indicated through movement and gesture.
  Shot of Frances looking with disgust at her mother.
  Close-up on mother's mouth chewing from Frances' point of view.

MRS FARMER Why aren't you eating your eggs?
FRANCES I can't when you chew like that.

MRS FARMER (*stops eating*) Don't tell me how to eat.

Mother starts eating again.

FRANCES You're driving me crazy.

MRS FARMER You're the one who's crazy.

FRANCES I never raised a red, white and blue chicken and then went on the radio about it.

MRS FARMER You're a traitor to your country. You and your left-handed friends.

FRANCES Left-wing, left-wing. Not left-handed. Oh, go fuck yourself.

MRS FARMER Don't you dare ever talk to me like that, you slut.

FRANCES Slut, slut. Who paid for this house – and what have you done with your life, anyway? What have you done with the money I sent you?

MRS FARMER Who did everything for you? Who raised you?

FRANCES I raised myself, and it wasn't easy.

MRS FARMER Frances, I'm not going to take this kind of talk from you. You're here in my care and you're supposed to be getting better. . . or. . .

FRANCES Better? Or what, Mama?

Frances rises to leave.

MRS FARMER Sit down, Frances.

FRANCES Who do you think you are, the Queen of England?

MRS FARMER Sit down.

Frances sits down.

FRANCES What now?

MRS FARMER Have some coffee.

FRANCES No.

MRS FARMER Have some coffee.

Mrs Farmer angrily pours the coffee into Frances' cup. She keeps pouring until the cup overflows and the coffee spills onto the floor and onto Frances. Frances screams, picks up the cup and throws it to the floor, breaking it. Then she bolts from the table.

MRS FARMER Where are you going?

FRANCES Out.

MRS FARMER Don't you dare have a drink, young lady.

FRANCES I don't have any money, do I?

MRS FARMER I know you.

FRANCES No, you don't.

Cut to:
Frances' hand opening her mother's handbag and grabbing some money.

Cut to: interior of Farmer house, night
Frances comes home drunk. Her mother has waited up, and is reading in the living room.

MRS FARMER You're drunk.

FRANCES Me? But I hate liquor.

MRS FARMER You're drunk and that's against your probation.

FRANCES   I'm as sober as the judge who sent me here.

MRS FARMER   You make me sick.

FRANCES   You made me sick. (*Almost to herself*) That's only partially true.

MRS FARMER   Go to your room.

FRANCES   That's fine by me. This floor show stinks.

Frances staggers up the stairs, and her mother goes to the phone and makes the call to the mental hospital.

Cut to: Farmer house, morning
Frances is asleep in her bedroom, hungover from the night before. The attendants from the mental hospital have arrived to take her away. They are with Mrs Farmer at the bottom of the stairs.

Cut to:
MRS FARMER   Frances. Frances, get up, Frances. Time to get up, Frances.

Cut to:
Frances hears her mother calling her and gets out of bed with difficulty. Finally, she walks to the door and opens it.

FRANCES   What do you want?

Cut to:
MRS FARMER   There's somebody here to see you.

Cut to:
Frances looking for something to wear. The floor is

*strewn with clothes. She chooses a dress and sits down
on the bed and falls over, sleepily.*

Cut to:
MRS FARMER   Frances, hurry up. They're waiting. . . .
    Frances?

Cut to:
FRANCES   I'm coming.

Cut to:
Mother and attendants, waiting.

Cut to:
Frances, dressed, walking out the door and shutting it.

Cut to:
Frances walking down the stairs.

FRANCES   Who's here?

*She walks to the bottom of the stairs. She sees the
attendants and yells. She runs back up the stairs and
is caught by the two attendants.*

FRANCES   No. No. You can't do this to me. (*Crying
    and screaming*) No, no. No, please. Don't.

The attendants are putting a straitjacket on her.

FRANCES   I hate you, Mama. I love you. Don't do
    this. You piece of shit. I'll get you for this.

MRS FARMER   Now, now, just calm down, Frances.
    They won't hurt you. It's for your own good,
    Frances.

Cut to:
Close-up on Frances as she screams and struggles.

The attendants carry her out. Her mother follows, picking up the shoes Frances has kicked off, holding them to her chest.

Cut to:
Close-up of mother's face seen through the bevelled glass at the top of the front door.

Cut to: interior of middle class home
A family is at the dinner table. It is Dr Taylor's home. His wife, daughter (teenaged) and young son (eight years old) are around the table.

DR TAYLOR   Stop fidgeting, Robert.

MRS TAYLOR   I told Mrs Stone that you might not be able to be there for dinner on Friday night.

DR TAYLOR   Yes. I've had a difficult week. We've been trying out a new drug on some of the patients. We've had erratic results. Some have been hallucinating even more than usual. You look different.

MRS TAYLOR   It's my hair.

DR TAYLOR   Yes, I see. But nothing seems to work on some of the patients. That Farmer woman. . .

Daughter looks up, briefly, then continues eating.

DR TAYLOR   . . . is still rebellious. A thoroughly unpleasant woman. Everyone hated her, you know.

MRS TAYLOR   Did they?

DR TAYLOR   Yes. The most difficult woman I've ever encountered.

DAUGHTER   That doesn't make her insane, does it?

DR TAYLOR   This does not concern you, miss.

DAUGHTER   May I please be excused? I have home-work.

DR TAYLOR   What's this I hear about your wanting to be an anthropologist? Mother mentioned. . .

DAUGHTER   I'm going to study anthropology.

DR TAYLOR   And who do you think is going to pay for that?

DAUGHTER   I don't know yet.

DR TAYLOR   It's dangerous work that will have you going to uncivilized places.

SON   Can I go?

DAUGHTER   Margaret Mead does it. Ruth Benedict.

DR TAYLOR   Margaret Mead looks like a man and divorced her husband.

Daughter gets up from her chair and begins to leave the table. She looks at her mother. Her mother smiles wanly and grasps her hand. Daughter walks out of the room.

DR TAYLOR Dear, we're going to have to do something about your daughter. Stop fidgeting, Robert.

Cut to: exterior of mental hospital.
Frances and nurse are talking.

NURSE They don't like me speaking to you.

FRANCES Are you going to get fired?

NURSE There's talk.

FRANCES No one can see me here, I mean, no one from the outside. Without you I'd have no news of anything. They're going after everyone.

NURSE Without you, I wouldn't have looked into all this. They've revived the Dies Committee, and they've named Odets as one of seventy-nine people 'active in communist work in the film colony.' The Dies Committee has become the House Committee on Unamerican Activities – something like that.

FRANCES Unamerican? Clifford must be terrified. He always worried about whether he had courage. Of course I'm spared that, being insane. If I were sane I wouldn't have told the truth. That's a good test of mental health. The ability to lie. Clifford lied to me. Hoover lies all the time. He's got the soul of a dogcatcher.

NURSE And he's so consistent. His first job was for Attorney General Palmer. Remember the Palmer raids?

FRANCES Too bad we can't purge him. Just kill the guy. I wanted to kill Clifford.

NURSE (*laughs*) I don't think I've ever loved anyone that much.

Frances walks into an overgrown garden.

FRANCES Not enough to kill him? (*Laughs*) I was happy with him – ecstatic, I think – if ecstasy means being out of one's mind – Yes, I was insane – but they wouldn't have thought so – For love we're expected to be laid low – My Dr Taylor would like that, insane by reason of love. A man can kill a woman when he's jealous. Isn't that so? (*Laughs*) But when I was my most happy, I was miserable, too. All I thought about was him. I was hooked on him. He called me baby. And I felt like I was his baby. I got lost in his arms. He said he was too dependent on me, but it wasn't true. I was dependent on him – for my pleasure and, I guess, my pain, but the two were inextricably linked. After a while I couldn't tell one feeling from another. That's crazy, isn't it? When feeling good and feeling bad feel the same. Maybe they're right to have me here. It makes me angry just to think about it – ecstasy. It's a trap. Like thinking in terms of good and bad, or evil. My mother talked about evil all the time. She said God didn't make evil, that it was an absence of good. Just an absence. Shall we never speak of evil. Is sex a sin? Because we can touch it. Flesh is weak.

Cut to: interior of mental hospital
The two psychiatrists, Taylor and Kraus, are discussing Frances' case.

DR TAYLOR I've been talking with Dr Freeman about the transorbital lobotomy he's developed. It's much simpler to perform than the prefrontal. He's seen Frances several times, and he says he's had great success with women like her. Freeman says that by severing the nerves connecting the cortex to the thalamus, he is severing those nerves that deliver emotional power to ideas.

Cut to: stills of mental hospital buildings

DR KRAUS (*voiceover*) The notoriety her case has caused us has neither been good for the hospital or the state. Her attitude toward America – that insolence – toward Hollywood, her mother – it's just the same.

DR TAYLOR (*voiceover*) She is too aggressive. And her language – my God, for a woman – if my wife spoke like that (*hesitates*), I'd commit her. (*Laughs*) Well, divorce her.

Cut to: backyard of Farmer house

Frances' mother is talking to herself as she weeds and walks around the garden.

MRS FARMER . . . But the way she talked, and her filthy mouth. Saying terrible things to me. About other people. Why couldn't she just be good? . . . Seeing her like that. . . She wanted to be taken seriously as an actress but no one took her seriously after a while, what with her drinking and carrying-on. They hated her, especially after the police caught her driving drunk in Hollywood, and she used abusive language. That's what they called it. That's when they sent her to me, finally. There was nothing else to do. It broughtshame on us all. When I slaved all my life to try to make her decent. I want her back now. I need her to take care of me and Ernest. The doctors said she'll be quieter now. More peaceful. She's all I ever had to call my own.

Cut to: mental hospital, conference room
Frances' last meeting/interview with the two psychiatrists before her lobotomy. Camera on Frances.

DR KRAUS (*voiceover*) To be honest, we'd very much like to see you cured and able to leave us. But it was reported the other day that you were uncooperative during hydrotherapy. . .

FRANCES One of the other patients was taunting me and. . .

Cut to:

DR TAYLOR Well, Frances, it's always one thing or another. You cannot function normally in society like that.

Cut to:

FRANCES There are survival tactics in here. And I'm a survivor. Sort of. You know I'm not like the people here.

DR TAYLOR (*voiceover*) She resists our help consistently.

FRANCES I don't want to take those drugs. And I don't want to have any more shock treatment. My hands shake most of the time.

Cut to:

DR KRAUS   As for your therapy we are your doctors. You are not adjusting.

Cut to:

FRANCES   To what?

DR TAYLOR   (*voiceover*) There's that temper again, that lack of cooperation.

FRANCES   I'm sorry. It slipped out. But I'm not crazy. I'm an alcoholic, I'm sullen, I'm a lot of things. I am not insane.

DR TAYLOR   (*voiceover*) You have severe problems, Frances, and you continue to act out, to be aggressive.

FRANCES   I want to start my life over. Out of here. I'm sure I could make it.

DR KRAUS   (*voiceover*) We're not sure yet that you've proved that.

FRANCES   I need the chance to prove it. When I get out I'll get a job and live alone, quietly.

DR TAYLOR   (*voiceover*) If you were cured you wouldn't want to shut yourself away from people. You'd want to resume your career or maybe have a family.

DR KRAUS   (*voiceover*) What she says shows that she remains anti-social.

FRANCES   Whatever you say, I'll do it.

Cut to:

DR TAYLOR   We can't take you at your word. You're not a normal woman.

Cut to:

FRANCES   Normal? (*Pause*) Why have you asked me here today?

DR KRAUS   You're being paranoid again. I think we're finished now, don't you, Dr Taylor?

DR TAYLOR   (*voiceover*) Yes. We'll review your case and make our recommendations to the Board.

The doctors begin speaking with each other as if Frances is no longer there. Finally, Taylor looks up and dismisses her again.

Cut to:

DR TAYLOR   You can go now.

Cut to:
Frances' face in extreme close up. Her eyes shut in slow motion. Freeze frame. Music in. Credits roll.

The 16mm independent feature *Committed* premiered at the Berlin Film Festival in 1984. It was co-directed and co-produced by Sheila McLaughlin and Lynne Tillman. *Committed* was funded in part by the Jerome Foundation and Channel Four (London).